Wild Fire

Rose Mackie

Dedication

With thanks to Therese, Christie, and Barry, my greatest supporters.

Contents

Chapter One

The Story So Far

I n the distant future, Earth has exploded into the galaxy and colonized dozens of planets. During the colonization process, humans realized it was easier to genetically engineer the humans to fit a new planet, than terraform an entire planet to their needs. This resulted in a diaspora of human-template species that work together as part of an Alliance, pooling their shared economic, social, and military power against alien species.

Falosia and Verit are two colonized human planets, each with different matriarchal societies.

Falosians are empaths, and the planet has a majority female population. Their few males are cosseted, petted, and adored, but are not viewed as suitable long-term partners. Many of the Falosians have become dissatisfied with this situation and seek longer term mates of their own, craving the closeness of a pair bond.

Verit is a predominantly male martial society, ruled over by a Matriarch and her council of Maman. In centuries past, Verit was at war, and the Matriarchs of the time decided to engineer the males of their species into feline hybrids. It worked better than anyone could have expected, but had many unforeseen consequences for the males, leaving them with berserker rage. Verit is organized into clans and are among the most feared warriors in the galaxy. The Maman rule the clans with an iron fist, bearing centuries of guilt and responsibility for their part in the engineering of their males, while the males revere their females, but resent them for their iron control.

The Verit birth rate is declining, and unless something can be done, their species will disappear within a few generations. It is believed by Verit that another planet, Svoboda, is the cause of their infertility. Svoboda is male dominated and has an open policy of resistance against matriarchal cultures.

Falosia and Verit have come together to co-sponsor a new colony, hoping that finding mates between them may help solve both their issues. A small establishment group from both planets, under the command of K'Dec Maral, has landed to start the colony building phase. It has worked better than either group could have hoped. Despite some initial social friction, the Falosians and Verit colonists blend well, and there have been two successful matings already in the first few months.

However, the colony has been plagued by problems from the start. There have been multiple instances of sabotage, both on and off planet, disrupting their supply chains and placing the lives of everyone on the planet in jeopardy. A saboteur was caught and interrogated and pointed to Svoboda as the cause.

The colony has also suffered repeated failures of communications and scanning equipment, due to localized interference. It was discovered that a rare mineral, Zyilan, exists on the planet, and is the cause of the interference. Zyilan is highly valuable. It has never been found in such large quantities before, and when word gets out that Zyilan is present, it will change the power structure of the Alliance, and the galaxy. The fledgling colony is entirely unprepared for the onslaught of thieves and pirates that will descend on their little backwater planet.

In investigating the Zyilan, the colonists also discovered the presence of an ancient sentient alien ship, Casti. The only thing more prized than Zyilan in the galaxy is ancient alien tech. They have had to go to great lengths to keep this under wraps, including keeping an Alliance envoy as their "guest" to prevent him from reporting the situation.

They have resolved to keep everything secret, while they gather evidence against Svoboda for the crimes against the colony, but the urgency is rising, and they cannot keep the envoy forever.

Chapter Two

Prologue: The Market

A creature shrieked. A long, undulating, wailing cry that raised the hairs on Lenora's arms. She raced through the market, dodging people and stalls, blades up. When she reached the corner where the shop was, she skidded to a stop, her mouth gaped in shock. Vordan stumbled back out of a doorway, crashing into a market stall. The stallholder puffed up its feathers and squawked at him in anger, shoving him off.

He landed on his ass on the tiled walkway in the piazza, covered head to toe in green goop. Out of the doorway emerged a giant insectoid. Its legs emerged first, green chitin shimmering with red highlights as they unfolded. Its upper body reared back, revealing a dark red maw rimmed in sharp chitinous ridges, dripping more of the green goo.

"Need help, Flyboy?" she called as she started wading through the tide of shoppers frantically trying to get out of the fight zone.

He laughed. The idiot *laughed*. "No, your ladyship. I'll be right there." He flipped backwards, into a crouch and trained a gun on the creature. She blinked. *Where, in the name of the Goddess, did he pull that from?*

He shot the creature's right foreleg, and it wailed again. Lenora clenched her teeth against the pain as the sound crescendoed, vibrating through her bones and making her teeth rattle. The remaining patrons in the market scattered.

Vordan snarled at it. "Now, tell me where he is."

It hissed at him, shooting another gob of goo at his feet, and swiping with a ridged foreleg. He ducked and shot the offending limb. "I'm afraid I don't have all day. I'm on a schedule. The only question is whether you run out of legs before I get my answers."

Five days earlier...

Chapter Three

Everything in Its Place

Lenora walked along the aisle of storage unit five, scanner in hand, surveying her domain. The shelves of the storage unit were stacked high with gray transport containers, their labels facing front, aligned with military precision.

Overlaid in her vision was her logistics view, detailing the contents of each box, its transport history, materials safety warnings, and more. With a flick of her eyelid, she dismissed the data, fed from the HUD control cuff on her ear. Everything was perfectly in its place, organized and calm. Just like she liked it.

She accessed her audio channel on her HUD, intending to call her team, when it beeped, and she realized she was receiving an incoming call. Blinking to accept, the K'Dec's face floated into view. Lenora took a breath. An unexpected call from the colony governor was never a good thing.

"Good morning, K'Dec."

In her usual clipped, efficient manner, the K'Dec responded. "Good morning, G'Dec. My apologies for interrupting you. Please make yourself available to attend a meeting at my office this morning at 1000."

"Of course, ma'am. May I ask what it is regarding?"

The K'Dec's eyes were bleak. "I have a mission assignment for you."

Lenora stilled and her heart dropped–she chose her words carefully. "A mission, ma'am?"

The K'Dec's visage softened a fraction. "Yes, Lenora. I'm sorry. You know that I had hoped we would not..." She trailed off, her voice firming. "Just come in for the briefing. We'll talk more then."

"Yes, ma'am." There was no other acceptable response.

The K'Dec nodded brusquely and signed off. Lenora lifted a shaking hand to lean on the nearest shelving unit, panic turning her legs to noodles. She turned to examine her neat storage units again. The cleanliness and order were revealed for the lie they were. What had she been thinking? That she could escape her past? That she could come to a new planet and fill her life with the calm serenity she so desperately needed. Wherever she went, her choices followed her, snapping at her heels like demons out of ancient mythology.

She stiffened, shoring up her internal defenses, shoving away her incipient panic and fear, bolting closed the door to her emotions by sheer force of will. She was a senior officer of the Falosian military–it was the single good choice she had made in her life. She had devoted her life to the service of her mother's planet, and if they required her to undertake a mission, she would. Whatever the personal cost.

She smoothed her jumpsuit uniform. There was still work to do before her briefing. Lenora placed the call to her second-in-command. The young Falosian officer's face floated in front of her, her yellow eyes bright with energy.

"Morning, Boss! How's the stock take going?"

Lenora laughed, feeling her spirits lift. Yulli had an innate gift for making those about her feel better, just by her presence. "I've completed unit five. Please let the team know they did an excellent job. Everything is present and correct."

Yulli bobbed her head in acknowledgement. "Great. That means we can start on unit six. I'll let MedBay know we are coming to them later on today to do MedBay stores-"

"Actually, if you could delay that. The K'Dec has asked me to attend a meeting this morning at 1000 and there may be an assignment for us. I'll let you know after."

Yulli bobbed her head again, blissfully unaware of the churning anxiety within Lenora. "Yes, ma'am."

They exchanged a few more operational details and pleasantries before signing off. Lenora took a last look around the storage unit, before stepping out of the airlock onto the waiting gantry and sealing it behind her. She crossed the open grassed courtyard that was the center of their small base, heading for the administration building. With each step, she couldn't help the sensation that she was walking further and further away from the small, happy slice of peace she had carved out for herself. That she was voluntarily putting her head back in the noose. She sighed. She had survived before, and she would again. It wasn't like it was the first time.

***

Vordan smiled professionally at the ground staff as they finished loading up the last of the equipment in the flyer hold. He repressed a sigh, thankful that this was his last trip to the agricultural station. He had spent all week doing little bunny hop flights to deliver necessary equipment.

It was essential, meaningful work, building the future of the new colony. He was contributing to the survival of his society, and he should be proud to be playing his part. Instead, he was mercilessly bored.

When the Matriarch had assigned him here, after years of flying for Verit in contract mercenary engagements, he had welcomed the adventure (not that she had sought his opinion on the matter). The thought of establishing a new colony, of finding a mate of his own, had sparked images of wild adventures. Of wrestling an unknown wilderness into submission. He'd done more combat flying in the past ten years than most did in their whole life. This should have been like an extended vacation.

Instead, he was stuck ferrying agricultural cargo back and forth, as part of a carefully laid out colony establishment plan that would ensure the safety, security, and success of the new venture. It was sensible and boring. What was worse was that once this phase was completed, he'd then be reassigned to ferrying building materials for the new homes.

The plan would be to rinse and repeat for the next fifty years or so, as new colonists moved to the newly named Dalat colony, and the colony expanded.

He sighed again and hopped into the cockpit of the shuttle. It was a solid craft, bulk produced all across the alliance, perfectly suited for colonial life. They could run for years with minimal maintenance, used commonly available parts, and were stable enough to carry livestock. A far cry from the sleek scout vessels he was used to. He began the pre-flight checks, seeing the sea of green indicators appear in his flight HUD, when there was a gentle ping indicating an incoming call. He blinked in surprise when he realized who it was from.

"K'Dec, is there a problem? Is everything alright?"

She laughed huskily, "Yes, pilot. All is well. I need you to attend a 1000 briefing. Are you available?"

Vordan quickly checked the time on the HUD view. "Yes, ma'am. I have one scheduled flight this morning to AgStationOne. I can be back before then."

"Thank you, Vordan."

He signed off, completing the pre-flight checks on automatic as his mind raced, considering the possibilities. He had rarely interacted with the K'Dec. As the commander of the base, she had many responsibilities, few of which intersected with flight planning. As he took off, he comm'd Lucius, First Warrior of the Dathalka clan, and the leader of the Verit warriors on the colony, as their Prime was off-world with his mate who was recovering from a long illness.

"Go ahead, Warrior," came the warm, gruff reply, against a background of repetitive thudding. He must be out at the building sites, where they were laying the foundations for the utilities complex.

"Luc, I've been asked to attend a meeting with the K'Dec this morning. Did you know? Do you know what it's about?"

"Yes and yes." The thudding ceased, followed by curses and shouts, and then more thudding.

"Care to share?"

"Nope."

Vordan considered. Luc was generally open with the males. It was unlike him to be so tight-lipped. "Is there anything I should prep for the meeting? Will you be there?"

Luc hesitated, and Vordan heard a rustle, and the background noise lowered. "Vordan, it's about an off-world mission. That's all I can say for now. Just be there, Warrior. You'll be fully briefed."

Vordan considered. "Acknowledged, sir. Thank you."

***

The rest of the morning passed excruciatingly slowly as Vordan completed his run. Eventually, he found himself sitting in the K'Dec's office, resisting the urge to fidget in anticipation. The others filed in, and he nodded politely as they took their seats at the table.

The K'Dec was already seated at the head, as expected. He made a couple of half-hearted attempts at conversation until Lucius-De, First Warrior of Dathalka, and Denara Pasal, the colony Chief Healer, and Luc's mate, arrived together. Both smiled at him in welcome. He grinned back, delighted to see them. They had been among the first of the Verit-Falosian matings, and every time he saw them, it gave him hope for his brothers and himself. If a smart, beautiful female like Denara would accept a stubborn, overbearing male like the First Warrior, there was hope for them all.

Next came G'Dec Lenora Pattra, their head of logistics, and G'Dec Sraya Rattan, their head of defense. The females nodded politely at him, taking seats at the far end of the long table, deep in discussion over a tablet.

The recently promoted G'Dec Zera Garrick entered. His interest was piqued–together, this group comprised most of the colony's ruling committee. The only people missing were the heads of administration and engineering, and the Maman, the female leader of the Verit colonists. The Maman was still recuperating after receiving an experimental alien medical treatment for a persistent degenerative condition.

"Thank you for waiting for me," came a clear voice, and Vordan whipped his head around to see Scara, a newly minted Maman. Just recently come of age, she had undergone her Maman birthright ceremony just two weeks past. The Verit males inclined their heads in a small bob at her, the females smiling at her warmly.

Vordan was surprised to see her here. Junior Maman often underwent years of mentoring before they were allowed to take on leadership positions. Still, he reflected, the entire colony was an experiment. Many things that were once taken for granted were turned upside down. He eyed her, considering. He did not know the young Maman well. He had only recently transferred to the Dathalka clan, after one of their own pilots had retired. While he had seen her at meals, they had not spoken a word. He sincerely hoped that she had a good head on her shoulders, and that he would not be ordered into folly by her inexperience.

The K'Dec nodded in welcome to Scara, clearly expecting her. "Thank you all for joining me on such short notice. I apologize for the urgency; however, we are on a tight timeline. This briefing is confidential. Highest security clearance."

Vordan started; he did not have the clearance for this. He glanced at Luc enquiringly, who shook his head and nodded at him to pay attention to the K'Dec. Excitement stirred. Whatever this was, it was big.

"I am streaming to your HUDs mission briefing files, and historic briefing packets. You may review them after we finish here to supplement this verbal briefing. You are here because the leaders of our worlds have made a decision. As you know, we have been subject to repeated sabotage attempts and incursions since we arrived on this planet. Two weeks ago, representatives of the Matriarch and the L'Kar met to discuss the new intelligence we have received, which indicates that the sabotage is the work of Svoboda."

Vordan snarled at the name of Verit's hated enemy, but he noted that no one else reacted. Clearly, he was the only one not already privy to this information.

"Our leaders have agreed to confront the Alliance with this—it is a clear breach of the alliance code, and if we provide evidence, they must take action. We need solid evidence to take this to the council. There are three goals. First, we need to know if this results from a splinter faction within Svoboda, or an action of the government. Second, we must know if this is part of a greater plan, and what the end goal is. Finally, we must know if they know that we have Zyilan and ancient tech on this planet."

Vordan's mind reeled, putting together the pieces of the last few months. The snippets of information he had come across, of hushed conversations. He had known there was something going on with the Alliance, but this... this was *huge*. This could mean war. It had been their biggest fear from the first moment the Zyilan was discovered, that someone would try to take it from them. Zyilan was highly valuable, used in everything from medical technology to stealth tech. When (not if) word got out that the planet had Zyilan, every mercenary, pirate, and petty princeling would descend on them. Their fledgling colony was not yet in a position to defend itself from an all-out assault. Their only hope was to delay the announcement as long as possible to allow them to fortify the planet against the inevitable.

"This is the mission. You will be split into two teams covering distinct lines of investigation. S'Daii Alliance Ambassador Amira has been working with the Falosian special forces, the Dagger Kiss, to trace where the saboteurs have been intercepting our supply flights these past months and has had a breakthrough. Amira will set up a decoy supply run. Odran-De and Zera will take Casti, and use its camouflage technology to mount an ambush, take prisoners, and trace them back to the source."

Vordan grinned ferally, excitement bubbling up. Casti was an ancient, sentient, alien ship they had recently discovered. It had bonded with Zera and had incredible capabilities that they had barely begun to understand. The scientists had actually come to blows over who got to study it first. He was disappointed that he wouldn't get the chance to travel on Casti, but the opportunity to actually use Casti in a real-life situation was beyond exciting.

The K'Dec continued. "On the way, you will drop Denara and Lucius off at Haven. Denara has been invited to speak on her most recent genetic therapies at a medical conference there. There are several prominent Svobodan officials going. She will see if she can pick anything up with her empathic senses."

"The last team will be Lenora, Scara, and Vordan. We know from the Malurien mercenaries that attacked Zera at the crater site last month that someone has placed several contracts for us on the Gray Market. Lenora will pose as a mercenary, take one of the jobs, and find out who is placing hits on us."

Vordan was stunned. He looked at Lenora, the logistics officer. She was so still, so self-contained. He couldn't imagine her posing as a mercenary. Her hair was jet black, scraped back into a tight bun, her skin pale as the moon. The only thing that gave away that she was Falosian was the classic yellow eyes, shining a warm sunny yellow, so at odds with her overall distant demeanor. She was a regal ice queen. Lenora looked back at him coldly, her glare daring him to say anything.

"Excuse me, ma'am?" Vordan raised a hand to speak. The K'Dec nodded in permission. "What will be my function on the team?"

The K'Dec raised an eyebrow at him, her lips quirking in amusement. "Vordan, you will pilot Lenora's ship wherever she needs to go. Lucius tells me you have extensive flight combat experience."

He flushed. "Yes, ma'am," he responded. "I have thousands of hours of combat experience."

"That's settled then."

"Thank you for the opportunity, ma'am. I will pilot the G'Dec wherever she wants to go and protect her with my life."

The corners of the K'Dec's mouth lifted again in the ghost of a smile that vanished before he could be sure that it had been there. "Thank you, Vordan. I'm sure Lenora will appreciate that."

Vordan risked a glance at Lenora, but she may as well have been carved from stone, he got so little response. The K'Dec moved to continue, but Vordan cut her off. "However, I have some concerns about this mission."

"Yes, Vordan?" The K'Dec was the image of patience, but Vordan could see Luc shaking his head at him from the corner of his eye. Realizing that he was pushing his luck, he smiled charmingly. It bounced off the K'Dec like peanuts off a wall.

"You may not be aware, but my previous clan, Tothas, is part of Verit's mercenary forces. We were an army for hire. I know how mercenary markets work, and they will never hire an unknown merc group of just three people." He saw Luc put his face into his hands. The silence drew out, and he realized that, charming smile or not, he may have crossed a line.

"Thank you for that insight, pilot. I am aware of your history. It is the reason we selected you. It will not be just the three of you; you will collect other personnel on the way. The details are in your briefing packet. As for Lenora being unknown, that won't be a problem."

The K'Dec looked at Lenora, who held her gaze for a long moment before nodding permission. "Before Lenora returned to her mother and joined the Falosian military, she lived and worked with her father's family. They are well known in this field." Vordan looked at Lenora with open curiosity as the K'Dec finished. "You will meet up with the Oonaugh Sect."

Vordan's jaw dropped. "The Oonaugh? Your father is *Oonaugh*?"

Lenora spoke for the first time in the briefing, her voice low and husky. It surprised him. The voice belonged to a jazz singer. It was lush and dark. Completely at odds with the military female before him. "My father is Dutak Oonaugh." The name fell into the silence.

"Dutak Oonaugh," he repeated incredulously. Lenora nodded, and he examined her again carefully before it clicked in his brain, and he was floored. "You are Lenorielle Oonaugh!"

Lenora nodded again, her skin ashen, her lips pinched tight. "I am."

He couldn't have been more surprised if she had declared herself empress of old Earth. "The same Lenorielle Oonaugh that did the IntGalOne raid ten years ago? That took on twelve Vranken class ships to run the trading blockade at Destiny? The Black Valkyrie?" Lenorielle was a legend, widely thought dead nearly a decade past.

"Yes." Her yellow eyes spit fire at him, daring him to speak further.

"You can exchange history later, Vordan. If I might continue?" The K'Dec spoke into the silence, and he flushed, remembering their audience.

He mumbled a polite, "Yes, ma'am."

"You have two months to undertake your missions."

This time the question came from Lenora. "What's the rush? An infiltration like this takes time and planning. I may have a reputation," she said glancing at Vordan, "but I've been out of it for years. There will be a lot of attention if I re-emerge without fanfare."

"The six-month colony establishment inspection is in three months. We must decide whether to declare that we have discovered the Zyilan and the tech or make other arrangements. If the Alliance is not implicated in the sabotage, or they take action against Svoboda, or if it is a small splinter group, we may choose to declare and trust in the strength and unity of the Alliance to work through this. If not, we may be faced with the choice of going against the Alliance."

"Secession?" Lenora's voice was tight.

"The possibility has been discussed." The K'Dec was noncommittal. "But we will not take such a drastic step lightly, unless we have obvious proof that the Alliance cannot be trusted."

"Why not just go to them now with our suspicions? They have their own investigators. Surely they could help us?" This came from Denara.

"Because the mercenaries that attacked the crater came on the same ship as the last Alliance Envoy. Until we know how involved they are, we can't trust them not to work against us."

Vordan nodded in understanding. The K'Dec returned her gaze to Lenora. "As for attention at your re-emergence, we're counting on it. A random merc could never hope to meet the leaders behind this, but your history gives you a certain cachet. We hope it will be enough to tip the balance in your favor and get you an opportunity to work your way up. We don't have time for a patient infiltration. This needs to be done in a single big splash."

Lenora pondered, tapping her fingers lightly on the table in front of her in an off-beat rhythm. "That's a big 'if.' We will have to offer Dutak something for his cooperation if we want his people to pose as my team. What do you have in mind?"

"We will provide you with a five-microgram canister of Zyilan. He doesn't need to know that it was mined here."

Vordan whistled low. Five micrograms of Zyilan was enough to buy a decent sized island, complete with mansion and servants, on a nice planet.

"G'Dec Sraya will stay here with me and run colonial security. The other reason for our rush is our little Alliance Envoy problem." The K'Dec looked at Vordan. "The Envoy has been our guest since the inspection two weeks ago."

He gaped, stunned again at the scale of the situation. "You took an Alliance Envoy prisoner? Kidnapping is frowned on in most civilized worlds, you know."

The K'Dec smiled tightly at him. "He is our guest," she repeated with a snap. "We cannot keep him here forever. Aside from us not having long term 'guest' facilities, he is a Malurien Royal. It's only a matter of time before someone comes looking for him."

Lenora finally smiled. It was faint, but it was there. It contained a ghost of humor. "We just keep stacking up the problems, don't we?"

"He has been accommodating so far, but it's clear he knows we are up to something. He is not happy that his Alliance mercy mission to deliver us supplies was used as a cover to land a paramilitary force, and he feels some level of responsibility for that, and is being cooperative for now. However, this goodwill will only last so long."

Luc chimed in. "Malurien are deadly, especially their royals. They are faster, stronger, more intelligent... I'm not sure we could contain him if he made a determined effort to escape. He could disappear into the bush and simply wait for the rescue to come. It's unlikely that we'd ever find him. It's a big planet."

"Why not just let him go?" asked Vordan.

"Because in every problem there is also opportunity. Should things go wrong with the Alliance... let's say that the Malurien Empire may provide a contingency plan." The K'Dec stood. "Take tonight to read your briefings. You leave tomorrow. Zera will drop you at each of your destinations in Casti."

Chapter Four

Journey

C asti was unlike anything Lenora had ever seen. Matte black, somewhere between rock and metal, with ridged striations covering its rear. It was a long cylinder floating in the air above the colony, completely camouflaged from sight and sound. You only saw it if it wanted you to. Vordan was piloting them up to Casti in a small flitter shuttle, designed to carry just a few passengers.

The briefing packet had noted that the ship was run by a sentient AI, and the ship was morphic - it adapted and conformed to its pilot's will.

"Welcome, Lenora, to *Hai-Zerran*." A soft voice spoke directly into her HUD feed, and she looked at Zera enquiringly.

"Casti is the name of the type of vessel. The Ulariv, the ancient aliens, named their ships after their operators. This one is Hai-Zerran, named for Odran and I." Zera reached over and stroked back the long silver hair of her mate, Odran, sitting next to her. They were the second Falosian-Verit pairing, and they were visibly besotted with each other. He squeezed her knee, looking at her with such open adoration that Lenora had to look away. That single look revealed the naked truth of their soul bond.

She couldn't bear to look at their joy. She loved Zera, the female was one of her closest friends, and she didn't begrudge her happiness, but jealousy bit deep. Needing a distraction, she replied to the ship. "Thank you, ship. How should I address you?"

She was astonished to sense the ship's amusement–she knew it was sentient, however this was an *actual* emotion that registered on her empathic senses. "However you like. Zera calls me Casti. If you prefer, you may do so as well. Casti means home, wherever you are. My purpose is to look after Zera and hers, to provide for anything and everything they might need."

"Thank you, Casti." Lenora looked at Vordan in the pilot seat. They had not spoken a word this morning. Had not spoken at all after his incredulous outburst at the briefing yesterday. She had been furious. She had never wanted to see that blend of admiration, fear, and excitement in a male's eyes again... but she supposed she would have to get used to it again. Despite her best efforts, Lenorielle's legend had continued to grow.

She steeled herself. She'd put up with it for the sake of the mission, even if it made her feel sick, made her itch to grab her knife and drive it into the eyes of the arrogant male who looked at her so boldly.

Lenorielle had always attracted male attention. They had always desired to possess her, control her, wanted to be the one to bring the notorious, vibrant smuggler to heel. She smiled grimly. More often than not, they had turned ugly when they realized she would never allow herself to be owned in any way.

Lenora had no such issues. Lenora was calm and contained. Her very ordinariness protected her, and in doing so, gave her a freedom that Lenorielle had never known. She had spent long nights reflecting on the irony that she had more freedom working in logistics in the military than she had ever had as the head of an intergalactic cartel.

The open shuttle bay loomed before them as Vordan expertly navigated the shuttle into place. As they gathered their gear, Zera announced that Casti had prepared a light meal for them, where they could discuss their mission in more detail.

Lenora followed Zera out of the shuttle and into the ship proper, stopping in her tracks when the utilitarian black and gray of the shuttle bay abruptly transformed into smooth wooden floors and high curved ceilings. As they walked, the walls were punctuated with large picture windows, open to an unmistakably Falosian view–black sand beaches and a dark blue and pink ocean.

At one opening the light green curtains billowed, and she realized it was doors open to a balcony. Stepping up to them, she scented the salt sea air and a hint of seaweed. "It's so real. How is this possible?" she murmured.

"It's Casti," came Zera's reply from behind her. She turned to look at Zera and noted that her gaze was trained on the horizon. "It's my grandmother's house on Falosia, in the H'Kada province. I spent my summers there with my sisters when I was young. It is the place that holds the fondest memories for me, the place I think of as home. Casti recreated it."

Lenora felt a pang of envy. "I didn't live on Falosia until I turned twenty-four, and I defected from the Oonaugh and located my mother. I grew up aboard ships, traveling between merc stations and trading posts."

"That must have been exciting, for a while." Zera's clear citrine gaze seemed to see right through her.

Lenora shrugged. "It was, when I was young and craved adventure. It took me a long time to realize that I wanted something different. Wanted to be different." She reached out a gentle fingertip to touch the wooden frame of the door. "I would give anything to have memories like this, of home."

Zera reached over and squeezed her around her shoulders. "It's never too late to make memories. You get to decide where you will make your home."

Lenora nodded. "I think Dalat could be a home, eventually."

"There you are then. Come on, let's catch up to the others. Until you make your own home, I don't mind if you share mine." Zera squeezed her shoulder affectionately one more time, then led her towards the dining hall. They had only gone a few steps when a creature screeched and launched itself from the shadows at Zera.

Lenora tensed, but Zera laughed in delight. "Hello, Bandit!" She reached down, and the creature leaped up into her arms. It was fuzzy, its fur dark red that lightened to pale gold on its muzzle, paws, and belly. Large black eyes in the front of its head sat over an elongated muzzle with fluffy circular ears that twitched and rotated. It reached out a long neck and sniffed at Lenora over Zera's shoulder.

"Ummm... hello, Bandit," offered Lenora tentatively.

Zera laughed as they walked towards the mess hall. "Bandit here found Odran and I when we were on the crater mission. He's incredibly intelligent and has adopted us. He likes it on the ship, and Casti spoils him endlessly."

When they reached the dining room, it was small and intimate. In a traditional Falosian style, the tables were low, with heavily embroidered jewel-colored cushions spread around. Everything was paneled in light wood, with colored lights illuminating fretwork from behind, casting rainbow shadows.

A vegetarian feast was laid out. Little bowls and platters contained dozens of different vegetable dishes. The others had already started, each piling their plates full from the selection in front of them.

Lenora dropped her gear off to the side and slid into place, eyeing the food with enthusiasm. "This looks great. I haven't had *tlacha* since Falosia. Where did you get it?" She picked up one of the stuffed roasted mushrooms and bit into it, making appreciative ooohs as the juices burst in her mouth.

"Casti can reproduce the foodstuffs from the genetic sequences we provided. It has also started growing some of my favorites from seeds we brought with us," responded Zera, as she handed a piece of shredded fruit to Bandit, who held it in his delicate front claws to nibble.

They ate in silence, exchanging small talk for a few minutes, before Zera spoke. "Where will you go to meet Dutak?"

Lenora considered as she chewed. "I am out of the loop. I don't know where their current bases are. My best bet will be to go to one of their public fronts and ask for an audience." She eyed the team around the table. "My father was not pleased with me for leaving the clan. He may well choose not to see me."

Luc shrugged. "We'll deal with that when it happens."

"The best option would be to go to Rilaz. There is a large spice merchant exchange in the south port. It is a legitimate business, but has also been used as a cover by my family in the past. I should be able to get a message to him from there."

"We'll drop Luc and Denara off at the conference first, in case we need to wait around for a response."

Vordan asked, "How will we get there? We can't arrive in Casti; we'll cause a riot. But if we arrive in just a flitter, it'll cause suspicion. They'll want to know where our ship is."

Odran smiled mischievously. "Leave that to us. We can't share all our secrets."

Denara looked at Lenora, compassion in her eyes. "What will you tell your family? They'll want to know what all this is for."

"The truth, up to a point. That I am running a mission that I need a merc cover story for, and we're willing to pay. They take all sorts of gigs. If I present it as an offer of a job, they might go for it." Her brow furrowed. "We will need to be very careful what we say. They are fiercely intelligence and highly trained. They have been the controlling cartel in this region for over one hundred and fifty years. If you give them even a hint of what is happening, they'll have your planet out from under you before you can blink." She looked at Vordan directly for the first time, and was struck by his Verit beauty. The Verit males were genetically engineered to be warriors, their DNA spliced with a cocktail of feline and alien DNA. They were a handsome people, colored in a palette of winter. With metallic hair fibers and pale skin, they often appeared carved from stone.

Vordan was true to type, with dark iron-gray long hair braided in their traditional style, and pale skin. Like all Verit, his jaw was subtly stronger and his cheek bones sharper than you would expect for a humanoid species, as a result of his humanoid-feline dental structures. He was beautiful. Judging by his outburst at the briefing, he was also an arrogant fool. He was probably used to the Verit Maman falling all over him and his beauty easing the way for him. "Try to contain your excitement and your runaway mouth. You must act as if you've flown with Lenorielle for years. These people don't take kindly to barbs and insults from newbies."

He bristled at her words and tone, as she intended. He had irritated her from the first, with his brash manner and handsome face, his childish romanticism and enthusiasm about her life. She wasn't sure why she was picking a fight rather than just ignoring the moron, but something pushed her to goad him.

Despite his raised hackles, his tone was mild in response. "Don't stab at me because you are afraid of seeing your family again. You're right, I don't know you. But you don't know me either. I spent a decade flying merc ships. Don't put your judgement onto me, my lady. Take your bad mood out on someone else." She hissed in fury at his response. He grinned at her. "What's wrong, princess? Not used to people telling the great Lenorielle off?"

She exploded. "How dare you! I am a military officer. I am not some spoiled kept lady!"

He leaned back, stretching lazily to deliberately antagonize her. "Then act like it. Stop throwing a tantrum."

She opened her mouth to scold him, when Lucius roared, "Enough!" She closed her mouth with a click, flushing in embarrassment. She had forgotten her audience. "You are both officers, and this is unacceptable conduct. You are dismissed for today. Take some time to cool off and find out a way to work together. This mission is too important for your bickering."

Vordan went to retort, but thought better of it when he saw Luc's expression. He swallowed whatever he was going to say. "Yes, First Warrior. My apologies G'Dec." He stood and bowed stiffly and marched out.

Lenora glared at Lucius for a long moment, daring him to order a G'Dec, before she noticed her Falosian companions. Zera was staring at her in astonishment, her face caught between amusement and incredulity at her outburst. Denara looked at her with open concern and shook her head slightly.

"Very well, I will retire as well." She grabbed her plate and walked through the door. She stomped through the corridors before she realized she had no idea where she was going. Gradually, as her temper cooled, she began to feel like an idiot. Lenora did not lose her temper.

Scratching at some male that insulted her was a very Lenorielle thing to do. It scared her how fast she was slipping back into her old habits.

"Casti, are you there?"

"Yes, Lenora."

"Where are my quarters?"

A pale blue light appeared at the bottom of the wall on her left. "Follow the light."

She wandered through the wooden corridors, getting increasingly lost. Inside Casti, it seemed like there was something just a little odd with the proportions. The ship seemed much bigger than it should be. Eventually, the blue light slid up the wall to outline a doorway.

She stepped through into a large Falosian room. The wood floors continued inside, as did the domed ceiling. In the center was a sunken fire pit, open on all sides with a circular bench surrounding it, covered in more of the jewel-toned cushions. The large low bed was set into a sleeping alcove in the corner to her right, piled high with comforters, cushions, and throws. It was a delightful, dark nest to sleep in. Access to a washroom lay on the wall to her left, next to a large entertainment screen with more floor cushions in front of the screen on layered woven rugs in pink, dark purple, and teal.

The most incredible feature of the room was the large picture window, which took up the entire wall opposite the door, leading to a balcony carved of light sandstone, overlooking the black sand beach and waves below. It was stunning.

Despite still being early in the day, she was exhausted. The past twenty-four hours had been a series of emotional upheavals she had been completely unprepared for. She had stayed up late reading the briefing pack and had not slept on the shuttle over. She eyed the washroom entrance. She was certain that a bath and a nap would significantly improve her mood. Grudgingly, she admitted she owed that flyboy idiot an apology. It was not his fault that she was angry and needed to vent. He had simply been a convenient target.

She moved into the washroom, delighted to see the deep carven stone tub. Yes, a bath and a nap would fix lots of things.

Chapter Five

Getting to Know You

Lenora was awakened by a knock on her door. She was deeply asleep, and the knock came from light-years away. She dragged herself out of bed to the doorway, opening it to find a bright-eyed and smiling Vordan.

"What?" she grumped.

His grin didn't budge. "Would my lady like to join me for breakfast?"

"Breakfast? We just had lunch."

He cocked an eyebrow at her. "Check the time. You slept eighteen hours straight. It's 0800, and we have a mission to plan."

She stood still in shock for a moment before her brain finally clicked into gear. Belatedly, she realized she was in the fluffy pants and oversized tee that she slept in. When she had emerged from her bath, her luggage had been waiting for her in her room.

Vordan was doing a good job of not grinning like a lunatic at her. Goddess knew what her hair looked like–it was tightly curled, and she usually wore it slicked back in a regulation bun to stop it going everywhere, but she had been so exhausted after her bath last night that she had collapsed into bed without doing her usual routine. She was fairly sure it had developed into a bird's nest on her head.

"Alright. Give me fifteen minutes."

He bowed formally. "I await the lady's pleasure."

She examined him suspiciously, but could find nothing but sincerity in his expression or emotional resonance. With a sigh, she shut the door and began prepping for her day. She clucked when she saw her hair—she didn't have time to scrape it into her usual style, so she settled for wrapping it up on top of her head with a pretty scarf she had. It wasn't exactly regulation... but then, they were traveling on an ancient alien ship to meet her family, where she was going to pose as head of a criminal cartel once more. She supposed regulations about the neatness of her hair were a low priority right now.

She dragged on her pale blue military jumpsuit and strapped her weapons belt to her waist. When she opened the door, Vordan was waiting in the hallway patiently, leaning against the opposite wall. She noted he had also changed his attire slightly.

The Verit males in the colony had realized that most of the females were vegetarian, and wearing their traditional manhood furs made them somewhat uncomfortable. They had taken to wearing just plain black jumpsuits. Away from Falosia, Vordan had taken the opportunity to wear what she suspected was more normal for a Verit male. A tight-fitting black leather vest over black cargo pants, with a knee-length fur trimmed overcoat. She had to admit that it suited him. The fur was a dark, dark green of an animal she didn't recognize. She snorted. With his braids and all the leather, he looked more like a pirate than she did.

The old Lenorielle would have loved him. Might well have dragged him to her bed. A fast-talking, charming, mercenary pilot clad in leather? Yum. But Lenora... she knew all too easily how fickle his type of male could be. How quickly they could drop you when they realized they couldn't get their way.

"This is a new look," she offered as he fell into step with her.

He jerked slightly, surprised at her comment, before preening. "You like it? I wanted to fit the overall look of the Oonaugh."

"It looks good on you," she replied. There was no need to lie. He knew he looked good. Probably thought he could sweeten her temper that way.

"Thank you, my lady."

"Why do you do that?"

"What?"

"Call me 'my lady'? I'm not a lady. Not when I was her, and not as I am now."

He looked at her strangely. "It's polite." After a long pause, he continued. "It says more about me, and how I treat females, than it does the female." He paused again. "Does it bother you?"

She gave his question genuine consideration, touched by his answer. "No, not really. But my family will think it strange. I would never have accepted it before."

"What should I call you then?"

She shrugged.

"My Goddess?"

She barked a laugh. "No."

He pretended to ponder, and she didn't miss the mischievous glance in his eye. "Your worship?"

"Nope."

"Let's see. Arrogant bearing, confident, in control... Queen? Pirate Queen?"

"Not a chance."

"Warlord? Warlady? Warperson?"

"You're enjoying this," she accused.

"Politeness is part of civilized society," he responded stoically, and she couldn't help laughing outright. "Seriously, what shall I call you?"

She stilled, then smiled. "My crew always called me *hulla*. It means 'in charge.'" He huffed, and she mock glared at him again. "But my friends and family called me Elle."

He smiled at her, delighted that she would allow him to use her clan-name. "Very well, Elle."

"I didn't say we were friends."

He snorted in laughter at her acerbic tone. They reached the dining hall in just a few minutes, and Lenora became instantly suspicious–she had wandered for nearly half an hour the night before. Perhaps Casti had decided that she needed a walk to cool off.

It was just the two of them. When they sat down, Casti produced another vegetarian meal for them. This time, a simple vegetable soup with bread.

"So, tell me what I should know about Lenorielle. What will they expect me to know?"

She shrugged. "Honestly, I don't know. I haven't been home in a decade. Its reasonable for people to change a lot in that time."

"Where did you grow up?" He seemed genuinely interested. His eyes lit up with curiosity that was distinctly feline.

"On Oonaugh ships and stations. Before my father became head of the clan, he ran their logistics. Moving all the cargo we traded or stole. I worked with him, and I was good at it. No one could get anything past customs like I could. My family on my father's side is huge, and we all worked for the clan. I have nine brothers and sisters, from different mothers and fathers. There are fifty-five aunts and uncles at last count, and hundreds of cousins."

Vordan paused with his spoon in midair. "Are you joking?"

"Nope. My father is Tritaura."

Vordan blinked, then carefully ate his soup. "Tritaura are not human-template."

"Nope, they are reptile descendent."

"How could he... you know... with your mother..." He looked so awkward to be asking her she laughed aloud.

"Tritaura are highly adaptable. They are gender fluid, and can breed with every known species. They also have a limited chameleon ability. They can't change some things, like body mass or brain organ composition, but superficially they can adjust their looks, body composition and gender to a species preference." He looked so abashed that she reached out and bopped him on his nose. "Don't be speciest, Vordan. The Oonaugh are so successful because they are composed of many different species. They harness the skills of all those that come to them. If you can't interact with other species, especially non-human template, then you should bail out now."

"No, no, you're right. I've got it. Just... did you inherit anything from your father?" He looked her over frankly, and she stiffened in annoyance. "You look Falosian."

"That is an inappropriate question, pilot, that you don't need to know the answer to. It is well outside the mission parameters."

His face went purple with embarrassment. "My apologies, lady. You are correct, it won't happen again."

She nodded solemnly, accepting his apology. "Tell me about yourself," she commanded, attempting to move away from more personal matters.

He nodded. "I am a Pa ranked pilot, Verit Warrior mercenary class. I am trained in ship-to-ship combat, and spent a decade in clan Tothas, who act as an army for hire. I have fought wars the length of alliance space. I am qualified to pilot any shuttle or small attack ship, up to a class three. I am also qualified to pilot Verit, Falosian and Alliance standard transport, freight and large attack cruisers up to class nine."

"Weapons proficiency?"

"I have master level certifications in energy and particle weapons. Verit males are also trained in blade work and martial arts."

"Good. Anything else?"

He grinned broadly at her and fanned out his hands. Large, sharp claws extended two inches above his fingertips. They did not grow from his fingertips, like in the entertainment reels, but appeared over them. "I'm an expert at hand-to-hand combat, too."

She examined them in wonder, reached a hand out to touch one, pulling back when she realized what she had done. He smiled at her and held out his right hand for her examination.

"They are incredible. May I touch them?" He nodded. She trailed her fingertips over his, noting the channels for the retractable claws behind his more human like nail beds. The claws extended over his human nails and sheathed them. They shone slightly, and as she lifted them up, she noted slightly metallic fibers in the nail structure, similar to those in his hair. "How do they work with your finger joints?"

"The tops of our fingers are slightly longer than normal for the human-template, providing space for the nail sheathes to sit in them. The nails curve around the bone, see?" He demonstrated extending and retracting his claws a few times for her. Once she saw them, she noticed the slight differences in the musculature and bones of his hands. It had been camouflaged by the overall largeness of Verit males.

"These are amazing. Even if you were disarmed, you would never be without a weapon."

He winced slightly. "Some of our enemies have become wiser over time, and there have been cases where they have removed claws or cut the tops of fingers off altogether. It is extremely painful, and not repairable by normal medical means."

She nodded again. "Thank you for showing me."

He smiled, pleased that he was back in her good graces. "Now you. Fair is fair. I want your story."

She supposed he was right. It was only fair. "Like I said, I grew up with Dutak on Oonaugh clan ships and stations, running logistics and evading customs. When I was in my late teens, we got ourselves mixed up in a clan war. One of our allies, Branauwen clan, started a war with a Galatean syndicate. It was brutal and bloody, and they were stupid to get involved with it. You can't beat Galateans on their own turf. Branauwen wanted our support. We were considering it—we really don't like getting involved in other people's wars, and we did business with the Galateans... but one of my father's sisters had married the Branauwen chief, and she was pressuring us to help them."

She stopped and took a long sip of her water to give herself a moment. "The Galateans gave us a little warning against getting involved. They kidnapped several members of my family, including my younger sister, Arielle, who is half-Galatean on her father's side. My father weighed up the options and decided not to get involved. It was bad for business. I thought he would negotiate for Arielle's release... but that was bad for business as well. He has lots of children, and he couldn't let the Galateans know that he would give them concessions every time they kidnapped us, or it would be open season for us all."

She swallowed against a surge of remembered fear. "He told Branauwen and the Galateans that he wouldn't get involved, to sort out their issues themselves. Then, he decided to bomb the Galatean base. To send his own message, that no one controls Dutak Oonaugh. No one manipulates the clan."

When she looked up at Vordan again, her eyes were burning with rage. "That rat bastard was going to bomb the base with his own daughter on board. My Ari. Ari is gentle. She was an artist." She laughed bitterly. "Father put her to work making forgeries–she was an expert at it, but her true skill was art. She could have been one of the greatest artists of our age."

She shook off her anger, pulling together the shreds of her composure. "I decided to get Ari out. I took my ship, the Black Sun, and a few of my friends and cousins, and we infiltrated the base. We found her. They had tortured her, beaten her, but she was alive. I brought her home and bombed the fucking base myself."

She scooped up a spoonful of soup and ate it with slow deliberation. "My father was so proud. He was the one that named me the Black Valkyrie. It was the start of my reputation. A true daughter of Dutak. Out of all his children, I was the one most like him." She couldn't help the bitterness lacing her words.

Vordan reached out and placed a gentle hand on her wrist. "You know that's not true, Lenora. I don't know you well, but even I know you would never sacrifice someone you cared about for a mission."

She forced herself to unclasp her hand from the spoon. "Perhaps," she replied noncommittally. "I worked my way up in the clan for years. Eventually, I just got sick of it. The people, the lifestyle, all of it. I found my mother. When I did, she was living on Falosia. She had retired. She was a bodyguard and a commercial negotiation empath. That's how she had met my father–she monitored a deal he was doing."

"Did you live with her?"

Lenora shook her head. "I could never forgive her for leaving me with him. She had her reasons... but too much had happened." She smiled. "I met Maral in my second week there, in a bar. I was determined to drink away my sorrows, and she found me hiding in a hole-in-the-wall selling cheap wine. She was the one that offered me an alternative path. Asked me to consider working for the Falosians. They needed someone with my skills. Eventually I told her who I really was, and she organized an Alliance pardon for me, in exchange for plying my very specific trade on behalf of the Falosians."

"Maral?"

"The K'Dec. She is my oldest friend. When she called and told me she had accepted the colony governor's position, I thought she was mad. I thought she was crazier still when she asked me to come with her. What the hell would I do in a colony?" She laughed again; this time light, not bitter at all.

"She saved me in so many ways. I found honor in using my skills to serve my planet. And I was ready to rest. The colony surprised me. I loved it. I love the ruggedness of the landscape, the challenge of building something from scratch, of making a life there." She sighed. "I thought I'd never do this again. I thought I'd buried Lenorielle for good. But when Maral asked, I couldn't say no. I owe her everything."

He reached over and took her hand, looking at her with admiration writ clear on his face. "I understand that this is hard for you, Lenora. But I think you might be one of the strongest people I've ever met. Once this is over, you can go back to the colony, pick up your life. This is only temporary." He paused. "If I've learned anything in a decade of fighting, it's that you can bear anything for a while."

She squeezed his hand gently in thanks for this support. She pulled her hands away and scrubbed her face. "You're right. Time to end the pity party for one, and put on my big girl pants."

He nodded, his eyes kind. She was touched. In her experience, kindness, compassion, and understanding were rare jewels to find in people. So unexpected in someone like Vordan. Perhaps she had judged him too quick, failed to see beyond the cocky flyboy surface.

"As for my skills. I am an expert in interstellar travel and interstellar negotiations. I am trained to command ship-to-ship battles, and in infiltration and espionage. Every port, every planet, I have contacts in. There is no-one I can't find, nothing I can't get through, nothing I can't procure if needed. Before I became the Black Valkyrie, they used to call me the fixer." She smiled grimly. "The Oonaugh do love their little code names." She smoothed her jumpsuit cuff. "I am best with long range energy and particle weapons, although Zera has been training me in Delma-Ley-At for years."

Vordan nodded appreciatively. Delma-Ley-At, the Falosian martial art, was perfectly adapted for a smaller female body mass. It was deadly when applied by someone with training, and Zera was an acknowledged master. She had recently begun training some of the Verit males as well.

Lenora looked down, realizing that she had finished her soup. "Thank you for listening. I haven't told the story in a long time. I think... that I've been trying to forget her. It's unsettling, the prospect of pulling her skin back on."

Vordan nodded again. "I'll be there with you. Whatever you need, just let me know."

Chapter Six

Rilaz

They reached Haven the next day, a Gen2 Alliance colony of the planet Nirvana. It was unremarkable in its imports and exports, but boasted more financial institutions per capita than any other planet in the Alliance, thanks to its extremely low tax rates and favorable trading legislation. The conference was being held in a large resort, and they waited nearly a day for their assigned shuttle window. The sky was dotted with hundreds of small craft flitting back and forth. When their assigned flight window finally came, Vordan piloted their shuttle down to the surface and back in less than an hour, dropping Denara and Lucius off at the plush shuttle bay attached to the hotel where the conference was being held.

Lenora largely avoided Vordan for the next two days. The unexpected intimacy of their discussion left her feeling exposed, so she resolved to keep her distance for now, until she could corral her surging emotions. She spent most of her time with Zera and Scara, brushing up on her martial arts training and refashioning her Lenorielle wardrobe with Casti.

Zera walked her through the Falosian-style corridors to Casti's fabrication room. The chamber was a smooth oval, in the featureless matte black that seemed to be Casti's default state. The materialization pod was in the center, with a low console with a screen off to one side.

"Casti, please enable Lenora's access to materialization design functions," instructed Zera.

"Confirmed, access granted. Welcome, Lenora."

Zera smiled at her. "I'll leave you two to it. Let me know if you need anything."

Lenora meandered over to the screen and tapped the green flashing icon. It pulled up a menu that she was unfamiliar with. "Umm, Casti, I don't know how to use this system. "

"You may simply instruct me what you would like, and I will develop a preliminary design for your review."

"I see. Is there anything that you can't create?"

"Many things."

"Can you be more specific?"

"Perhaps you could tell me what you want, and I will tell you if I can make it or not?"

"I need attire, weapons and some technical devices."

"That should all be feasible. Let us start with attire."

"I think you and I are going to be excellent friends, Casti." Lenora took a deep breath. "Alrighty. I need..."

***

They reached Rilaz the following day. Odran summoned them to the control room, which proved to be a circular chamber with a raised gantry and 360 degree viewing walls.

Odran wasted no time in explaining their plan. "When we reach Rilaz, Casti will cloak. We will be undetectable by any technology we are currently aware of. We will generate a fake trail to suggest that a cloaked Malurien vessel passed by and dropped off your shuttle, in case anyone comes looking. We can stay here for several days. Casti will communicate with you via HUD channel." He paused, looking pained. "Casti has teleportation capabilities. In a pinch, we may be able to teleport you out. But you should know, we haven't really tested it and do not know its limits. We'd also like to keep the tech secret for now, so if you need to teleport, best not to do it in public if you can."

Lenora and Vordan looked at each other in delight. "Teleport? Like, actual beaming technology?"

"Yes. Like I said, it's *a secret*."

"Right. Acknowledged. A secret," responded Lenora, still grinning. There was a long pause, and she elbowed Vordan, who hid a laugh with a cough. "Um, yeah. Confirmed, not a word."

Odran looked to the ceiling, muttering a prayer to the Goddess for strength.

"Do you need anything else?" asked Zera.

"No, Casti fabricated everything I needed. The ship is a marvel. I just need to change and grab my gear from my room."

"Best do that now, then. We'll be there in ten minutes."

"One more thing." Lenora looked at Scara, who had been silent throughout the exchange. Scara looked uncomfortable with the attention. "I will stay here."

Lenora raised an eyebrow at her. "May I ask why?"

"Surely you must have wondered why I was sent on this mission. I am hardly the first pick for espionage." Lenora nodded. She had wondered, but it wasn't her job to question orders. She had to admit that she had been concerned about the young female among the Oonaugh clan. "I have specialist skills that will be of use when we are hacking the Svobodans."

"You're a hacker."

Scara smiled grimly. "I can hack anything. I believe the word they keep using is 'prodigy.' I would be a liability in this phase of the mission, so I will stay onboard until I'm needed. I have been trained to run data and intel for operations."

"Very well. Thank you for letting me know. We will be in touch through comms."

Lenora nodded to everyone again and spun on her heel. Honestly, it was a relief not to have to worry about Scara. It was one less thing on her plate to deal with. With every step she took, her legs became more leaden. She had been resisting turning back into Lenorielle for the longest time. With the prospect of changing into her clothes, it suddenly seemed very real.

She reached her chambers and looked at the outfit she had left on the bed. A far cry from her military jumpsuit, Lenorielle had gone for dark and dangerous.

The outfit comprised of dark red leather pants and jacket woven through with syn-armor threads that shimmered in the light. Under the jacket she wore a reinforced black tank that laced up the sides, designed to give her movement while fighting. Over it all flowed a black *raugh*-skin jacket that absorbed the light and was impervious to scanning. In addition to making it harder to see her body outline, and therefore harder to shoot her, it had particle weapon deflection technology and billowed in the slightest breeze. It looked decidedly impressive.

She sighed as she pulled the garments on. Her younger self had been very dramatic. She had soaked up the attention that came with being the Black Valkyrie, had commanded respect and fear wherever she went. Half of the trick was projecting confidence and assurance, and this outfit conveyed that in spades.

Next to don were her boots. Thick soled with a solid grip, they clipped up the sides to just under her knees. The thick soles had low level anti-grav plates sewn in. Not enough to actually fly, but enough to give her an edge in maneuverability, speed, and lightness in a fight.

Finally, she pulled on her headpiece. The black, gem studded circlet wrapped around her forehead and down behind her ears. While it appeared decorative, aside from having a whole host of useful tech, it served the more prosaic purpose of taming and holding back her wild mane of hair.

She stood examining herself in the full-length mirror, turning this way and that. She smiled slightly to herself. Ok, she had to admit that she looked good. She looked like the avenging Valkyrie from the old stories that she had been named for.

She strapped on her weapons belt. The finishing touch was to let down her hair. Lenorielle had been incredibly vain about it, and had spent hours and a truly obscene amount of credits on oils, creams, and treatments. She snorted at the folly of her younger self—one particularly intelligent adversary had actually nearly succeeded in killing her by tracking her spending and determining her preferred shampoo, and poisoning an entire shipment in an effort to kill her.

She took a deep breath and took out the tie, shaking free her mane of hair. It curled and twined in a million spirals down to her butt. The weight laid heavy against her neck, instantly making her sweaty, and the thought made her laugh. *Suffer for beauty, Elle,* as her Melati had always said.

She shook off the remaining melancholy as she grabbed her bags and strode towards the shuttle bay, constructing her armor in her mind as she went.

When she stepped into the bay, she heard the wolf whistles before she saw the others. Zera, Scara and Vordan were standing next to a small, sleek flitter. Zera whistled again, "Damn, female! Why were you hiding that hair? It's glorious!"

Lenora smiled. "Thank you. I hide it because it's a complete pain in the ass to maintain."

"It's amazing." Vordan smiled, his eyes drinking in her entire form. "You look every inch the pirate queen, Lenora."

She laughed. "My father read stories to me from Earth, about pirate queens. I so badly wanted to be one." How she regretted her childish folly. "Call me Elle. Best get used to it now."

He nodded and bowed gallantly. "Ready to come aboard, my queen?"

"You got it, Flyboy." She winked at him and dropped her pack at his feet, flicking at it with a finger as she sauntered past. "Bring the bags."

Scara sniggered at them, and Vordan guffawed. "Yes, ma'am."

Zera embraced her. "Take care, sister. Don't lose yourself again."

Lenora hugged her back tight, fear clogging her throat. She swallowed convulsively. "I won't. I know who I am." It was a promise to herself as much as Zera.

Zera pulled back, her eyes solemn. "Are you sure? We go through lots of incarnations of ourselves in life. Perhaps this will help you find your next one." The moment drew out before she smiled wickedly, throwing a glance at Vordan loading the bags. "But have some fun doing it, ok? That man is fiiine and you look like the Goddess herself." She slapped Lenora playfully on the butt as she danced out of range, her laughter glittering in the air. "Be safe."

Lenora nodded a last time and entered the flitter. She settled herself in the passenger seat of the small cockpit and awaited her pilot. Instinctively, she sat with the military bearing that she had adopted these past few years. She clucked her tongue at herself; she had to be smarter than that. She leaned back and slouched, swinging one leg over the armrest in practiced indolence.

***

When Vordan entered, he noticed the change immediately, but wisely kept silent. He had been stunned with Lenora. *No*, he thought, *Elle* had emerged in her pirate queen outfit. Gone was the contained, controlled military officer. She had been replaced with a stunning, raven-haired vixen, with eyes that shone like the sun, and skin pale as the moon. He could easily see her leading her team on a raid. Even the way she moved was different. It disturbed him, the ease with which she could change herself so completely. Left him wondering who the real female was.

The trip to Rilaz was short, both of them contemplating the journey ahead in a surprisingly comfortable silence. Their only communication was when she directed him to a specific landing terminal in the southern port. He followed her out of the ship, leaving their things onboard for now, into the chaos of the concourse. Rilaz was a planet composed entirely of markets. Everything conceivable could be bought or sold here, and from where he was standing, he could see dozens of different species.

The concourse was wide, with a high, glass-domed ceiling above terraced shopfronts. The ground level was filled with food vendors of every style, with the goods increasing in price and rarity as the levels increased. His feline senses were stunned by the mixture of aromas from the food, from the chatter of thousands of different voices and languages. "Keep a hand on your valuables at all times. Most clans train their children here at the port," Lenora murmured, and he nodded in return. He had already noticed the groups of tiny children running fleet-footed through the crowd.

"How far away is your family's business?"

"Not far. They are just outside the port, three streets to the south." She took off, striding through the crowd with confidence, head held high, and he trailed in her wake, observing how people instinctively scurried out of her path.

"Do you think you'll be recognized?"

"Of course. I suspect someone has already alerted my family that I am here. They control this entire region. They—"

"ELLE!" a voice screamed over the hubbub, and the crowd parted to reveal a tiny female running towards them. He tensed to defend as the female launched herself at Lenora, who caught the smaller female in a bear hug and spun her around. As she did, Vordan saw the diaphanous wings, the overly large jewel-colored eyes on her delicate build, and blinked. The female was Galatean. He had never seen one in the flesh before. They were highly popular on the intergalactic entertainment net for their grace, beauty, and incredible mimic abilities.

"Ari!" Lenora cried as she clung to the smaller female, who hit at her with tiny balled fists as she cried and laughed at once.

"You bitch! Where the hell have you been? Ten years, ten years with only the odd message, and then you just stroll into the port like nothing has happened!"

"I'm sorry, I have so much-"

Ari cut her off, talking over her. "Do you know how hard we looked for you? Mother turned the sector upside down!"

"I know, I know, I'll explain-"

"You'd better have a good explanation, or Melati might murder you herself!"

Lenora laughed and disentangled herself from the female, placing her on the ground. Vordan noted the hulking males that had encircled the two females as they greeted each other, each with the typical hard eyes and over-developed musculature of bodyguards.

"Care to introduce us, Elle?" he enquired.

Both females turned to look at him, and the little one's eyes went wide. "Oh, Sister, he's delightful." She practically purred, stroking a tiny finger along his green-furred lapel. "Is this why you've come back? You've brought your mate home to meet the family?"

He was too stunned to respond, her forward manner so unexpected. Lenora laughed again and pulled the little one's hand off him. "I'll explain everything to Father. This is Vordan. Vordan, this is my sister, Arielle."

He flashed her a charming smile and bowed elegantly, and she chuckled in response, sounding like little bells ringing. "Sister, you'll have your hands full with this one. He's entirely too charming for his own good."

Arielle turned back to Lenora, and in a blink, she changed. Gone was the sweet, joyful female, and in its place was a tiny queen. "Now, Sister, tell me why you have come back." Her voice was iron.

Lenora blinked at the rapid change. "Like I said, Ari, I'll explain to Father."

"Dutak is not here. You will explain to me. I run the south port now."

Lenora's eyebrows shot up. "When did that happen?"

Arielle smiled tightly. "You didn't think we'd all just stay as we were when you left us? We are not dolls to be put back in the closet when you don't want to play with us. Your leaving left a big hole in the business. We all had to take on other duties. This is mine."

"I see. I'm sorry, Ari. I didn't realize."

Ari laughed again, but this time, the smile didn't reach her eyes. "Why are you sorry, Elle? I like my work, and I'm good at it. Our operations have expanded five times since I've been in charge. Now, this is the last time I'll ask. Tell me why you are here. If you won't answer, you'd best get back on that pretty little ship with your pretty male, because you won't set foot out of the port without my approval." There was no give in her voice, and Vordan was certain that she meant it. He eyed the nearest bodyguard, who smiled at him with a mouth full of crocodile teeth, daring him to try anything.

"I have a job. A proposal for the Oonaugh."

Ari raised an eyebrow. "Really? I heard you joined the *military* on Falosia." She nearly spit the word, her voice dripping with disdain. "What does the Falosian military want from the Oonaugh?"

"I will only discuss it in private, Sister." If Ari's voice was iron, Lenora's was pure ice. The sisters eyed each other for a long moment, the tension palpable.

"Is that it? You came all this way in person just to make us a job offer? We do have comms, you know. You could have just called. At any point in the past *ten years*." Even Ari's poise and anger couldn't hide the hurt in her voice, and he saw the barb land with Lenora.

He saw her calculation, saw her consider how much to say next. Lenora turned to him, an apology in her eyes. "No, that's not all," Lenora replied. She reached over and took Vordan's hand and pulled him to her. Instinctively, he slid his arm up to her shoulder, wrapping himself around her. "You're right. I wanted to introduce you to my mate, Vordan."

Vordan froze for a split second, shock dashing through his system, before his brain caught up with what was happening. He smiled charmingly, leaning his body into Lenora, following her lead.

Ari stilled for a long moment as she looked at them both, her eyes widening. "Really? You finally let some male catch you?" Her eyes filled with tears, and Vordan was shocked when Ari embraced him, peppering his cheeks with kisses. He was going to have whiplash. Things were changing too fast around him. "This is wonderful. Welcome to the family, Brother."

"Um, thank you." He eventually managed to put his hands on her shoulders to push her away. She clapped her hands in excitement.

"We must celebrate." She turned and motioned to a guard, who peeled off from the others and began moving through the crowd. "Let's head home. We can talk business and introduce your male to the family."

They followed her to a side door to the concourse and found the male she had sent ahead sitting in a small open-topped hover vehicle. They piled inside, and before Vordan knew it, he was sandwiched against Lenora and a bodyguard as they sped above the Rilaz markets in the bright sunshine. Below them, the fabric-covered awnings changed colors as they moved through the different zones, and the warm breeze playfully tugged at his hair.

"We aren't going to the spice merchants?" Lenora asked, and he saw Ari shake her head.

"No, we outgrew that years ago. We took over the *Louten* temple on metal hill." Ari looked at him. "Metal hill is where the jewelers are. It's lovely. The temple has plenty of space for us. It's an enclosed compound."

They traveled over the planet, the smells and sounds overpowering. He felt the tension thrumming through Lenora where her arm, hip, and thigh were pressed against him. She was strung so tight; he was afraid she would snap. He reached out and patted her knee, and she clamped her hand down on top of his in a white knuckled grip, before she gradually relaxed her hold, gently braceleting his wrist.

When they arrived at the temple, he was disappointed. It was a long, low, single-story building at the top of a hill in a quiet area. The sandy colored stone was elegant and timeworn. He wasn't sure what he had expected, but from Ari's brief description, he had thought it would be a hive of activity. Not this slightly faded historic elegance.

His shoulders prickled, and he turned to see the females watching him.

"Well? What do you think?" Ari asked.

He examined the structure again. "It's charming," he replied.

"But?"

"But nothing." He shrugged. Lenora and Ari exchanged a glance and burst out laughing. For the first time, he saw the similarity in the sisters that their exterior differences had hidden. "Ok, spill. What's the trick?"

"What, don't you think we live and work in this 'charming' home?" Ari asked innocently.

Lenora rolled her eyes. "Stop teasing, Ari. Come. Let me show you one of our secrets."

Ari snorted. "It's not that much of a secret."

Lenora aimed a playful whack at her, and Ari danced out of the way elegantly, slightly lifting off of the ground as she fluttered her gentle wings for maneuverability. She led the way up the deep, shallow curved stone steps and opened a small carved wooden door, set into a giant set of double doors. "Welcome to Temple, sister. May the Goddess bless you."

"As the Goddess wills it," came Vordan's automatic response, and Ari whirled at him, her eyes squinting.

"I knew it. You're Verit! What clan?" she demanded, her fists on her hips.

"I am Dathalka now, but I was Tothas."

Her eyes glittered, and she turned to Lenora. "Wait until Mother hears you mated with a Verit. Her head might explode."

Vordan felt his stomach sink as he looked at Lenora. Would their ruse make the mission more difficult? Did her family hate Verit? She smiled faintly at him and shook her head in dismissal of his query.

"Welcome, new brother, to the Goddess Louten Temple." Ari walked them through the antechamber into an open courtyard soaked in sunshine, and his jaw dropped as he approached the railing. Falling away before him were terraces marching down the side of the mountain. The temple was built into the crest, and hundreds, no, *thousands* of personnel scurried like ants along the walkways. As far as he could see, the temple was a series of interconnected chambers, courtyards and gardens linked by a lacework of bridges, stairs, hover platforms, elevators, and pathways in elegant tiers.

Lenora walked up to the railing and stood with him silently, her eyes taking in the view. "Did you know?" he asked her.

She nodded. "We used to play here as children. But this..." She turned to Ari and held out her hand to her sister. "I am so proud of you, Ari. This is incredible. So many people..." She was stunned.

Ari squeezed her hand back. "Thank you, Elle. You have no idea how much it means to me to hear that from you..." She blinked rapidly, her jewel eyes wet with unshed tears. "Come on."

She led them down a pathway, through a courtyard and down a winding series of paths and corridors. Before long, he was lost, and he began to appreciate the tactical brilliance of this location. Even if it was breached, the chances of someone finding a way out were minimal. Eventually, they reached another double set of doors.

Ari looked at them, flashing a smile one more time, and threw the doors open dramatically.

"Oonaugh. One of our own has returned to us." She moved aside and dragged Lenora by her arm into the light of the chamber. There was silence for a moment, like the world held its breath, before the room erupted in shouts, comments, shrieks.

Vordan was in shock. He had never seen such a diverse group of beings—there must have been nearly thirty people, each of a different species, lounging around in the enormous area. The room was dotted with sofas, small tables, and desks, somewhere between a family room and an open plan office. Central to it all was a circle of large floor cushions around a long, low table.

The inhabitants moved towards them, and he snarled, the sudden movement, unfamiliar territory and unfamiliar people spiking his adrenaline for a fight. His claws snicked out, his fangs lengthening, hormones flooding his body, making him ready for battle, increasing his speed and strength. The red rage descended, and he fought against surrendering to the dark stranger within. The dark stranger that lived in all Verit males, the stranger that fueled their most protective desires and instincts.

He dropped his bag and fur wrap, and leaped in front of Lenora, snarling at the attackers, ready to defend his female or die trying.

"Oh, yeah, and she's brought her new mate," chimed in Ari from somewhere outside the doorway. "He's Verit."

The inhabitants froze when they saw him, and he felt Lenora's hand run up his spine to settle at the nape of his neck. Her fingers entwined in his hair as she pressed herself against his back.

"It's all right, Vordan. They are my family. They won't hurt me." Lenora's words were the barest breath against his neck, raising the hairs down his spine, and then turned his head to her fractionally, indicating

he was listening. "Be calm. There is nothing to protect me from here."
She stroked again, her fingertips tracing the shell of his ear down his
neck. He leaned into that touch for a moment, soaking in the gentle
fire as he allowed the dark stranger to be soothed.

"You are wary. There is danger here," he countered, his voice still
mostly a growl as he struggled to speak past the rage. In her closeness,
he could feel the tension still thrumming through her, as it had from
the moment she had glimpsed her sister.

"There is," she agreed. "But not in this moment, and not the kind
you can defend me from with claws. Please don't harm my family."

He finally looked at her, saw the pleading in her yellow eyes, and
nodded once. He straightened from his defensive crouch, retracting
his fangs and claws, but staying in front of her, keeping a wary eye on
the people before him. Daring them to come closer. Communicating
with his stance that she was *his* to protect. Her family stared at them
curiously for a long moment.

"Holy shit, that's hot. Where can I get one?" came a hushed voice.
Vordan looked at the speaker, blinking in surprise to see a large Es-
kethien male, all blue skin and metal implants, smiling at him viva-
ciously. The male raised a hand and wiggled his fingers at him.

"Mhhm. I wanna climb him like a tree," came another voice, and
their audience cracked up laughing. He felt some of Lenora's tension
drain away, but she stayed pressed against his back, wary. The move
looked casual as she leaned on his shoulder, but he could sense that
she was unsure of her next step.

"Second removed offspring, blood of my blood. It has been a long
time." The voice was just above a whisper, primeval and grinding.

The audience parted to reveal an ancient, bent Tritauran female
shuffle towards them. She was so old, her scales were dull and matte,
and her eyes were pale orbs, blind in her cragged face. Lenora froze

for a second, before her composure broke and she sank to her knees. "Melati," she whispered, and the tiny ancient one stepped forward and gathered Lenora into her arms, crooning to her as she rocked her. "You have returned to the nest. The stars are right in our world again."

Lenora clung to the elder. "Mela, I wrote to you so many times. Why did you never respond?"

The elder hissed at her, hurt and anger warring in her expression. "You *left*, Mela. You sliced us out of your life without a word. It took us two years to find you again. You do not get to leave, but still have the net of family to catch you when you fall. There are consequences to actions, child. Family is not a coat you can put on and discard at will. We are Tritau, the nest and root for our river of blood and life in this world. We are strongest together." The elder patted Lenora's face, taking the sting out of her words. "There will be time for that later. Why have you returned?"

Lenora sighed and dashed the tears away from her face. "I have a business proposal for the Oonaugh."

The elder cocked her head to the side, considering. "We will hear you." She turned and began her slow, painful journey through the group. "Come, Elle. Bring your male. Join us in the circle." She paused. "Everyone else, skit. You can gawp and catch up later."

As if by magic, the group dispersed, but Vordan caught many curious looks thrown their way. Within a minute, there were only six people left, sitting on the cushions around the low table. Ari helped the elder to sit, then sat by her right hand. An older male with a Malurien appearance, red skin, and large black horns, sat next to Ari.

On the other side of the elder, a middle-aged feathered female sat. Next was a younger male creature. He was bright orange, with red and yellow striations covering his skin, and a second, vestigial pair of arms with short claws on his chest. Vordan had never encountered the species before.

Last was a creature that was so stunning he could hardly look at her. It. He was unsure. It was silver, head to hoof. Bright, shining silver, as if dipped in paint. Its head was bald, and the eyes were pure white, each individual eyelash looking like tiny, silvered feathers. At the top, it appeared humanoid and vaguely female, wrapped in beaten black leather armor. From midsection down, feathers appeared, forming a dense silver and gold downy pelt. The legs were sat back on the hips, forcing the torso slightly forward, ending in wicked silver hooves. Wrapped around the legs were an assortment of belts carrying pockets of various items.

Taking his cue from Lenora, he kneeled on the floor cushion opposite the elder. Lenora took a deep breath, and he could see her attempting to regain her composure, to rebuild emotional armor after all the shocks of the day.

"Clan Oonaugh. I have a business proposal for you from Falosia."

The orange male made a skittering noise, and Vordan realized he was rubbing the claws on his vestigial arms together. Lenora looked at him, her expression shuttered. "When I want your opinion, Brother, I'll ask for it."

The male cocked his head at her, baring fangs in a grimace. "Still a cocky bitch."

To Vordan's surprise, Lenora grinned. "Takes one to know one."

The male's grimace widened into a grin. "Nice to see being a military drone hasn't dulled your edge, Sister." A muscle ticked in Lenora's cheek, but she didn't respond. "Last I heard, you were running logistics on some backwater bum-fuck nowhere planet. I knew you'd get bored."

She ignored the comment, her eyes refocusing on the elder. "I have a proposal. Will you hear it?"

The elder stared into space, considering, and Vordan waited patiently. Eventually, the elder spoke. "We will hear." She placed a hand on Ari's arm. "Ari, convene the clan. All sect leaders to attend tonight at 1900."

He felt Lenora jerk, but her words were polite, considered. "I would prefer a private hearing. This is a matter of planetary security."

The elder laughed, a rusty sound. "The hearing will be private. The council is to introduce your mate to the clan. You didn't think you could just waltz back in with a mate, and that we'd just accept him on your say-so? If he wishes to mate an Oonaugh daughter, then the clan will meet him."

"Can't that wait until—"

"I have spoken. Ari, make it happen." The elder groaned and slowly got to her feet, aided by those on either side of her. "I must rest. This is too much excitement for my old bones. We will hear your petition tonight after the clan meets at 1900."

Lenora reached to grab his hand under the table, squeezing it for support. "Yes, Mela."

Ari stood, her arm around the elder. "Luta, will you show our quests to quarters in the red wing? And organize some food, please." Ari cast a hard look at Lenora. "It is good to see you, Sister. Do not wander in the complex. Do not impose on our good will. You are an outsider here."

Lenora squeezed Vordan's hand again, and he felt the blow that her sister's words had struck. Lenora nodded in response, saying nothing. The silver creature motioned for them to follow, and it led them through the winding passageways until they entered an enclosed garden.

Luta pointed to a line of red tilework across the threshold of the garden entrance and spoke in a sibilant hiss. "Thissss marksss the entransse to the red zone. You can travel freely in there. Do not crosss the threshold without permissssion."

Lenora remained mute, so Vordan responded. "Thank you, Luta."

The creature nodded and ushered them into the garden. Inside, the garden comprised a series of rock gardens, shallow pools spilling into each other and little seating areas. It was lovely, clearly designed for calming serenity. Around the perimeter were wrought-iron gates. Luta led them to the third gate on the left and opened it with a push to reveal a smaller garden within, just small succulents and a stone bench under a bower, and a little cottage. "I will sssend food."

Lenora didn't respond again, and Vordan wondered if she was in some sort of shock, the emotional upheavals of the day catching up with her. He smiled again at Luta. "Thank you."

It nodded but said nothing further. It passed a long look at Lenora and raised a bright silver palm to her cheek. It didn't touch her, simply held the palm a hairsbreadth from her skin.

"Welcome home, Elle."

Lenora blinked rapidly, her eyes wet. Finally, she responded, her voice husky with pent-up emotions. "Thank you, Luta."

It nodded and spun on a hoof to stomp away through the gate. Lenora stared after it aimlessly for a long period, lost in thought. Cautiously, Vordan touched her shoulder. "Shall we inspect our quarters?"

She sighed and nodded and allowed herself to be guided inside. The cottage was comfortably furnished. The furniture was plush and low to the ground. A small sitting area, around an entertainment screen, and a curtained off alcove for a gigantic bed with about a million pillows and blankets.

On the opposite side from the alcove was a tiny kitchenette and next to it a door which presumably led to bathing facilities. Everything was in a simple dark smooth finish and the predominant décor was dark blood red, with yellow accents. It gave the overall impression of warmth and comfort.

Lenora stood in the middle of the room, looking lost.

"Are you ok?"

She nodded.

"You don't look ok. What can I do to help?"

She blinked and focused on him. "I... I just need to process. I never thought I'd be here again. It's hard seeing them all... and weirder being in guest quarters rather than family quarters." She sighed and ran a trembling hand through her hair. "I think I need a minute. I just need to process it all."

"Alright. You rest, I'll scout out the gardens and the wing."

She nodded again, and on automatic moved to the sleeping alcove. She began to divest herself of her weapons, boots, and coat.

"It's odd. They didn't take our weapons," Vordan mused.

Lenora shrugged. "They will have scanned us as soon as we walked in. They'd have taken anything they felt they couldn't easily neutralize, but as a general rule, they don't bother. It sends a message."

Vordan understood, "Bring your weapons if they make you feel safe. We are so powerful, we don't care."

Lenora nodded as she sighed and fell into bed in just her leggings and loose tank. "It's the same reason they won't bug these cottages or install surveillance in our rooms." She snuggled down into the covers.

"Seems arrogant and dangerous."

She snorted a half-laugh. "Oonaugh is arrogant. It has caused us problems before, and most likely will again. There is a fine line between pride and arrogance. But often, in clan interactions, confidence goes a long way."

Vordan stood in the doorway. Before he left, he hesitated and turned back. "I could have used a little warning about the mating thing."

Lenora felt instantly guilty. "I'm sorry to drag you into the ruse... but I didn't see any other way. I know Ari. She meant every word. She would have tossed us out on our ass."

"It's alright, I don't mind. I just would have appreciated some warning." He smiled at her. "Can we visit my mother and brothers next? Seems only fair if you introduce me to your family, I get to introduce you to mine. She'll have a conniption that I've mated with a non-Verit, and my brothers will be deathly jealous. It would be worth the hassle, having to sneak into Tothas security, just to see their faces."

She sniggered. "Seems only fair, my *beloved*."

He snorted out a laugh and left her to her contemplation. "Get some rest, pirate queen."

***

Lenora took her time, splashing water on her face and then sitting in the resting alcove, meditating. When Lenora next awoke, it took her a few moments to realize where she was. She was warm and cozy, bundled in quilts. A gentle glow filtered in from the curtains, and gradually awareness returned. She was home. After years away, she was back with the Oonaugh. Her eyes snagged on the red trim on the curtains. Not home, not really. Relegated to a red wing, an honored guest.

Still in bed, she stretched deliciously, postponing getting up and facing the mess of her life for just a few moments longer. How tempting to stay in this warm nest and just float back to sleep. The sleep had helped in one aspect at least; she was calmer. She had thought that she'd been prepared to meet her family again, but seeing Ari and her Melati after so long... It had hit her like an avalanche.

She wasn't sure she would have got through it without Vordan beside her. The idiot flyboy had been surprising. Charming enough to win over her grandmother... and willing to defend her against her entire family. Even Luta liked him. They had deigned to speak to him, and Luta didn't like anyone. Instantly she was swamped with guilt for misleading them all, for dragging Vordan into this farce of a false mating. She sucked in a breath, controlling her respiration, squashing the incipient panic attack. She would not fall back into the darkness. She had a job to do.

There was a rustle of cloth, and Vordan stood before the slight opening in the curtains. "Are you alright?" His voice was hushed in the alcove's dimness.

She nodded, focusing on her breathing.

"You don't sound alright. I can hear your heart racing." She glared at him, and he held his hands up in defense. "Don't look at me like that. It's not like I can turn my ears off!"

She didn't respond, the blood roaring in her ears as waves of panic and guilt assaulted her.

"Can I get you anything?"

She squeezed her eyes shut and shook her head. She just needed to ride it out, ride the wave... She felt the bed dip, and then he was next to her, lying on top of the covers, hauling her into his arms. She struggled to get away, her legs tangling in the covers, when he shushed her and tucked her head under his chin, pulling the covers up to her neck.

"Hugging releases oxytocin, which helps reduce stress and anxiety. Just lie here for a minute. I won't do anything, I promise." He slowly stroked his hand down her hair and her back, his palm a big warm weight on her spine. He repeated the motion again and again, and with every stroke, she felt the tension slowly dissipate.

By the time he finished, she was boneless with pleasure. She finally found the will to speak. "That feels amazing."

She felt his amusement. "Everything I do is amazing."

She disentangled her hand to give him a half-hearted whack. "Why does this help?"

"I told you; pressure helps. It releases oxytocin."

They lay there in silence for a bit before he asked, "How often do you get these?"

She stiffened, considering how to respond, before deciding to tell him the truth. "Not often, not anymore. It was worse before." She snorted a laugh. "Heading a criminal cartel was a high-pressure occupation, you know. They don't release 'Seven tips to reduce your cartel stress' articles in the intergalactic magazines." She sighed. "Thank you, but I need to get up. I'm starving."

He let her go, but he could feel the reluctance. "Are you sure?"

"What, you think I should just stay here wrapped up in your arms? Can't stay in bed forever."

"We could try." His voice was conversational. "I think I could give staying in bed with you forever a go."

The outrageous flirtation had its desired effect, startling a laugh from her. "I need to find my pack with my things. I need a brush. Goddess knows what my hair looks like."

He smiled, his teeth a flash of white in the dim light. "It looks beautiful." He reached out and tugged a spiral, laughing wolfishly when it sprung back with joyful abandon. "It looks happy. Why do you slick it back so much?"

She shrugged, suddenly shy at the unexpected vulnerability. "I'm a military officer. It's protocol. And the stuff gets everywhere. It's so much work."

He mock-leered at her. "So that's a no to staying in bed forever then?"

She leaned over and tapped him on his chest. "Come on, lazy. Let's get up. Aren't your species meant to be hunters? Go hunt me some food."

It was Vordan's turn to stretch, his claws edging out slightly as he did. She tried her best, she really did, not to look at him. Not to trace the curve of his lean muscles with her eyes, but damn, he was gorgeous. Lean defined muscles covered in smooth skin. "We are a feline genetic derivative. Haven't you spent any time around cats? Sometimes, we just want to lie in a dark comfy spot."

Her eyes narrowed. "I'm more of a dog person."

He surged up and caught her by the nape of her neck, bringing her nose to nose with him in an instant, and her breath caught at the power implicit in the move.

"Liar." He bared his teeth at her in a mock snarl, and Lenora rolled her eyes in response.

"Fine, I'll go get food without you. Don't bitch when I bring back all vegetarian."

He winced, letting her go. "That's just mean."

"Yup, that's me. You're stuck with a mean ole pirate queen turned military officer. Poor lil' flyboy, so hard done by." She grabbed her pack from where she had spotted it next to the door and sauntered into the bathroom, casting a slashing glance at him as she closed the door.

He laughed aloud. "Perhaps we should get you a caffeine drink. You're prickly when you wake up."

She picked up a discarded throw cushion and tossed it at him, delighted by his playfulness. Amazed at his ability to have laughter dancing through her after a panic attack.

***

Lenora stood in the bathroom, examining herself. Her hair wasn't too bad. A little combing and oil and she'd be fine. The outfit though... if her whole family were here, there would be a dinner. Her father would want to hold court. She sighed. Dressing up was the last thing she wanted.

As she went through the ablutions, she accessed her HUD. Sure enough, there was a message from Ari. "Elle, Dutak will return tonight. She has ordered a feast of welcome at your return, and to celebrate your mating." Ari paused, and Lenora could feel her choosing her words wisely. "I expect our parent will wish to welcome your mate into the family the traditional way."

Her blood ran cold, as Ari continued. "I'll send you a couple of outfits that you left here in your closets. Hopefully, they still fit."

Lenora checked the time and realized they had less than an hour left–she had slept the day away. She opened the door. "Vordan, are you there?"

"Yes, lady?" He was all seriousness, responding to the change in her tone.

"Do you have any ceremonial or formal clothing with you?"

He nodded. "I wasn't sure where this assignment would take us, so I packed for several contingencies."

"Good. My father is throwing us a ball to celebrate our mating." He nodded, not giving any hint of his true feelings. "I'm so sorry, Vordan, I wish I'd never said it now... Dutak will want to parade us to the family. He may wish to spar with you–it is traditional for Tritaurans to undertake ritual combat when a new member joins the clan, in order to determine their place in the hierarchy."

He nodded again. "I will be fine. I will try not to harm your father."

Lenora sighed. "It won't be as easy as you think. He's fast, smart, strong, and sneaky. He's headed up an intergalactic cartel his entire life." She reached out to Vordan, placing her palm on his arm. "Please be careful. It's usually just a ritual... but I've been gone so long, and he was so angry... I don't know how he'll react." She cursed. "I'm so sorry again."

He smiled grimly and placed his hand over hers. "Stop apologizing. It is done and can't be undone. Do you still think it was the only way to get us in?" She nodded. "Then it was necessary for the mission, and we will do whatever is necessary for the mission."

She searched his gaze, determined to root out any hint of deception or anger, but both her heart and her empathic senses told her he was completely serious. How unexpected. His generosity of compassion, and his commitment to duty. "Alright, thank you."

She stepped back and looked around the room some more, spotting a package next to the front door. "It appears my sister had some dresses dropped off while we slept."

Vordan looked like he had been slapped. "That's impossible. I would have heard them. Or smelled them."

Lenora laughed. "Maybe not. I keep telling you not to underestimate them."

Lenora grabbed the package and pulled out the options, erupting in curses when she saw what Ari had sent.

"What's wrong?"

"My sister thinks she's funny."

"Why?"

Lenora sighed. She had no other options. "You'll see."

"She seems to care for you very much."

Lenora sighed. "Dutak has many children spanning the decades of his life. Ari and I were the only ones close in age in the compound. We were very close growing up."

"Who was Ari's mother? Is she still with Dutak?"

Lenora looked at him strangely, then shook her head slightly. "Sorry, I forgot you don't know the history. Dutak is Ari's mother–he was female when he conceived her. Ari's father is a Galatean trader. He has never been in the picture–I'm not sure that he even knows Ari is his child."

Vordan looked so stunned that she patted him on the cheek. "It's ok, if you aren't Tritaura it takes some getting used to. You know my Melati that you met earlier?" He nodded. "She prefers the female body but was Dutak's father because the partner she fell for at the time preferred the female form, so she took the male form to let them have young."

There was a faint chime, signaling half an hour until they had to go. "We can discuss xenobiology and alien reproduction another time. I need to get ready."

She grabbed the outfits and dove back into the bathroom. She had to get this right. She had to convey just enough of the woman she was so that they empathized with her, but enough of the "new" that they didn't try to steamroll her as a daughter of the house.

She regarded the dress. The old Elle would have worn the skimpy outfit with pride, enjoying the attention and the admiring male gazes it drew. Oonaugh clan attire was best described as sensual, liberated, chic. The new Lenora wouldn't be caught dead in that thing, pre-ferring practical clothing. Even when she had joined her mother on Falosia, she hadn't adopted the Falosian dress standards, which tended to the form fitting and elegant.

She stilled. Why was this such a big deal to her? She'd certainly worn this and worse during her mission assignments. *Because this is you,* her subconscious whispered. Yes, that was it. She wasn't hiding behind an assumed identity for this mission. This was her, with her family, working for her new planet. She looked at herself in the mirror. Really looked at the female she had become over the decade. Was her controlled life enough?

She sighed, shaking her head. Goddess, she was as melodramatic as a Galatean soap opera. Perhaps, just for tonight, she would let herself be who she wanted to be. Not what her family wanted, not worried about fitting in with Falosian society, or complying with military standards. Just herself.

She looked at the outfit options again, considering. Yes, that would work... she grabbed the scissors from her travel pack.

Chapter Seven

Dinner and a Show

S he emerged twenty-five minutes later, and Vordan was nowhere in sight. She strode through the living room and considered her guns for a moment. It wasn't done to wear guns, particle weapons, or lasers at dinner, but she really didn't want to go unarmed.

She heard Vordan return, and turned to ask him about his weapons, when she caught sight of his face. He was blanched with shock, staring at her open mouthed. Her heart fell.

"What's wrong with it? Don't you like it?" She looked at herself in the tall mirror next to the door. "I thought it looked nice." She had combined several of the outfits provided by her sister into a single look. The bottom was loose, shimmering, dark-green silk pants, with large slits up to the hips on each side revealing morphic reptile design jewelry which twined up her thighs, constantly moving and shifting. Her father had bought her that jewelry when she turned eighteen, as a reminder of her Tritauran heritage.

On the top, she had taken a black corset from another outfit, shot through with silver and jet thread. She layered it with a short, shimmering black and silver pauldron and collar piece which had a high stiffened collar made of whorled silver designed to look like metal lace. It looked regal and had the added benefit of protecting her neck from attacks. Her hair she had twined up into a high crown, jet beads woven through her hair. They caught the light when she moved. In her hair, she had hidden a couple more morphic jewelry pieces that slowly shifted, looking like tiny lizards peeking out from her curls. To most mammalian species, it would be highly disquieting, but to Tritau it was high fashion. Her booted heels were black, but high enough to qualify as dress shoes without being uncomfortable.

The outfit presented as sexy, confident, mature, and regal. She had wanted to look like the pirate queen Vordan kept calling her, and she felt that she'd nailed it.

Vordan clapped his mouth shut with a click, his brow furrowed. He prowled towards her, moving to stand behind her as she looked at herself in the mirror. He loomed a hairsbreadth away from her, his clawed hands reaching for the silk pants on her hips when he paused. "May I?"

She met his eyes in the mirror and gulped at what she saw there. The intensity seared her to her bones. She nodded once, slowly. The tension stretched between them. He reached out, the calluses on his hands snagging slightly on the silk as he stroked the fine material. She shifted imperceptibly, and the pants split up to her hips, only the barest scrap of material keeping her covered. He groaned and laid his fingertips on the coolness of her exposed skin. "My lady, I just know I'm going to have to kill some idiot for trying to touch you tonight."

She met his eyes again. "Try not to. If they aren't family, they'll be clan, and it'll be problematic. We'd have to pay the death price for it."

He smiled darkly. "It'll be worth it."

"So, you like it?"

He froze for a second, slowly releasing his hands from her hips. "I love it. Every inch the pirate queen. Just remember that you walked away from them. They are peasants."

"Peasants whose help we need," she reminded him. "Dangerous peasants."

"Ok, I'll admit, as an analogy, it needs work."

She laughed, the searing intimacy of the moment broken, despite that she could still feel the warmth from his palm on the skin of her hip. She turned back to her guns and sighed. "I don't enjoy going in unarmed. All I have are my hair pins. I can't take any of the other weapons I brought."

"What's allowed?"

"Anything that's not a laser, particle, or projectile firearm."

"Wait." He went to his bag and started rummaging, emerging with two items. "Try this."

One was a woven back leather holster, with a tiny bejeweled dagger in it. The other appeared to be some sort of wire.

She took the leather holster. "This is lovely work. Where did you get it? Who is it for?"

He flushed bright red and shuffled slightly. "I made it."

Her eyes shot to his, wide in surprise. "It's lovely. You are a gifted artist."

He beamed. "I've always enjoyed weaving and crafting. I enjoy working in leather as a medium. The dagger was for my sister."

"I didn't know you had a sister!"

He smiled crookedly. "Why would you? I actually have two. My mother was blessed by the Goddess. This was for Fardi, the youngest. If we got a moment, I was going to send it to her. She has just passed her Maman ceremony. She wouldn't mind if you borrow it for tonight. She'd want to help a sister."

Lenora accepted it gratefully, touched. She held out her arm for him to attach the holster to her bicep.

"What is this?"

He grinned broadly when he looked at the bundle of wire. "Ah, I do like this. I got it on IntGalTwo, the last time I was there, from a most unusual alien. Watch." He unrolled the wire and flicked his wrist. He pronounced an alien word she had never heard before. The wire flattened and clicked, and he held a long ribbon of curling metal that buzzed ever so slightly. He looked around and pointed at a small coffee table. "Is that valuable?"

"No."

He nodded and swiped the wire at the table. Where it hit, the table dissolved. The molecules simply broke apart. "It's undetectable until activated, and is not particle, laser, or projectile. It is inert until activated."

She grinned. "I love it. Show me."

They spent a few minutes practicing before he declared she was competent in the weapon, and he showed her how to return it to its inert state. "How should I carry it?"

He motioned for her to raise her arms, and he wrapped the wire around her waist. In its inert state, it looked like an unusual belt. "This doesn't feel safe."

"It's perfectly fine. It's designed for covert use."

"You won't be saying that when I cut myself in half."

"Have some faith, lady."

"And remember, you must call me Elle. They'd expect it."

"Don't worry, Elle. We've got this." He gave her a wink.

"Oh Goddess, we're doomed."

He turned to his own pack and pulled out a long black coat, which he shook a few times. He pulled it on over his own plain black pants and shirt and turned to her. "What do you think?"

He was stellar. His iron gray metallic hair shone against the black on black. She fanned herself theatrically. "Who was it you said needed defending tonight? My clan mates will be all over you."

He chuckled, and they wandered companionably into the night. The air had cooled, and the garden was full of shadows and secret places. She felt Vordan tense in awareness before he relaxed when Ari stepped out of the gloom. "Taken to hiding in corners, Ari?" asked Lenora.

"Just testing your reflexes, Sister." Ari's face was full of mischief before she smiled sadly. "You'll need it tonight."

Lenora studied her sister as they fell into step. "That bad, huh?"

Ari nodded, remaining silent. Lenora couldn't resist reassuring her. "Don't worry, it'll be fine." Ari glanced at her in disbelief and Lenora nodded at Vordan. "He's here to protect us."

Ari looked at her and cracked up laughing. "You've never needed anyone to protect you in your life, Elle. I can't imagine you starting now."

"I think I'm offended," Vordan quipped, and Ari eyed him appreciatively.

"He has a sense of humor, at least." Lenora snorted to hide her laughter.

"At least?" Vordan was mock outraged. "Have you seen my biceps? I'm a *pilot*. On most planets, I'm considered a pretty good catch."

"Yes, yes, of course you are, dear." Ari patted him on the arm condescendingly and danced out of the way of his clawed swipe and dramatic snarl of rage with tinkling laughter. "Bit touchy though, Sis."

"You're enough to drive anyone to violence!" she retorted.

***

They reached the hall just in time for pre-dinner drinks. Her father had not yet arrived, so the start of the evening was spent waiting for the other shoe to drop. They were assembled in a large dining hall, with fifty of the senior members of clan Oonaugh, most family.

Some seemed genuinely happy to see her, with many stopping by to welcome her back. In others, she sensed dark, old resentments and jealousy. Yet more were suspicious, and those she watched most closely when they came under the guise of friendship, their calculating enquiries brittle and bright against her empathic senses as they probed for information. The swirling, churning emotions gave her a headache.

Vordan handled it with grace, much better than she did. He smiled politely, flirted just enough to be charming, and loomed convincingly when the time called for it. She had to admit, they made a good team. Even in all the mass of emotions, no one suspected that their relationship was fake.

He was solicitous, his gaze following her when she spoke, laughed, and moved. Wherever she went, he was there. A solid, warm presence. She had to admit, she could get used to the feeling of having him on her team. It was a dangerous comfort. Once this mission was over, they would go their separate ways again. She could not allow herself to rely on his, or anyone else's, strength.

They were just starting to eat when her father arrived. He strode into the hall without fanfare, his movement gliding and dangerous despite his advancing years.

"Daughter-mine. You have returned to the clan. And you bring a guest."

Lenora controlled her instinctive panic and anger and stood to greet him. "Yes, Father. This is Vordan. We come with a business proposal."

Her father nodded absently, his bright green eyes examining Vordan like a bug under a microscope. Oh no, this wasn't good. She'd seen that look before. She stepped in front of Vordan, forcing her father to look at her. "We would like to discuss the proposal." Protecting him with her body.

Her father didn't miss a beat, hissing at her, a rattle deep in his throat. "You know better than that, Lenorielle. Family always comes before business. You disappear, you don't write, you don't call... then you come back with an unknown male." He finally met her gaze, and she swallowed. He was furious. "You, my eldest female. Who said that she would _never_ mate." His eyes fixed on Vordan over her shoulder, and she felt him come up to stand behind her. "We must get to know your mate. You know we don't do business with people we don't know."

"You know me!" she argued.

Her father's gaze was fixed. "Do we? I wonder." He held her gaze for a moment longer, his slitted eyes unblinking. "Fortunately, this is not the Oonaugh clan's first time with this quandary. We have established traditions for this."

She blanched, fear making her light-headed. "Father, please, we don't have time for this."

He cut her off. "Then we don't have time to hear your proposal."

"But..." she responded weakly.

He bared his teeth at her. "You are in my house again, Daughter. You will comply or leave. There is no third option."

Lenora looked at Vordan, the question clear in her eyes. He straightened and stepped forward. "I would be honored to take part in your traditions, sir. But my lady is right. We are on a timeline. Is there a faster option?"

Her father weighed his sincerity and grunted, grudgingly impressed by his forthright and respectful manner. "Very well. Some things can't wait. We will do Suthakar tonight. If you pass, we will hear your proposal after."

Vordan bowed, clamping his right arm over his chest. "Thank you, sir."

Her father grunted and turned back to the audience. Their watchers had given up all pretense at decorum and were straining to listen. He roared at them. "There will be a Suthakar tonight! Our Elle would like her mate to be accepted into the clan. We welcome the mate of our daughter and will do him the honor of competing with our best."

His eyes roved over the assembled clan members, assessing them. Huge, scarred, a variety of species... his gaze settled on a hulking form. "Gruarg shall represent clan Oonaugh."

The assembled clan members roared their approval. The creature was huge, mottled dark green and purple, with large tusks jutting forward from its jaw. Dutak spun back to Lenora and Vordan, his eyes glinting in excitement. He examined Vordan closely. "The choice of weapons is mine." He paused for dramatic effect. "I choose bladed melee weapons."

Vordan nodded once and bowed again. He looked at Gruarg, who glared at him from across the hall, and smiled in a wide, arrogant grin. He leaned against the table, all relaxed arrogance. "I accept." He winked at Gruarg, who glowered at him harder.

Her father chuckled, appreciative of the sass. "Half an hour to prepare."

Vordan turned to her and held out a hand, and she was conscious of all eyes on her. "My lady, would you dine with me? It appears we have half an hour before our evening engagement. Time for a quick light meal, I think."

She bared her teeth at him in an approximation of a smile. If he survived tonight, she would murder him herself. "Of course, beloved." Didn't he know not to goad her father? Gruarg was a straight up murderer.

She allowed him to lead her back to her seat and fill her platter, aware of the noises in the hall slowly returning to normal. Her sister slid into the seat next to her, and under the guise of filling her cup, whispered, "I have to admit, your male has some sass. He's crazy, but he's got style."

She nodded, afraid to respond that she might not be able to hide her anger and churning fear for him.

Vordan slipped in beside her, placing their shared platter down. He draped an arm over the back of her chair and leaned in. "Tell me of this Gruarg. What species is he? How does he fight?"

Lenora unclenched her jaw. "He isn't a species. We aren't sure what he is. He might be an engineered being. He is a killing machine, perfectly adapted for it. He is physically strong, has incredible stamina. His skin is impervious to most weapons. Father screwed you with Melee weapons–a blade will never get through his skin. You'd need a particle canon to make a scratch."

He held up a piece of bread in offering to her. "What weapons does he have? Claws, fangs? Is he trained in blades?"

She nodded in thanks, and he applied a spread to her bread as she responded before passing it over to her. "He's a meat grinder. He prefers axes or hammers. One hit is usually enough from him."

She accepted the bread and deliberately took a bite, controlling her churning stomach.

"Is he a strategist?" Vordan picked up a piece of fruit and nibbled on it, giving every appearance of relaxation.

"No. Like I said, he's a grinder. He has one strategy, to beat into a pulp." She finished the bread and picked up a spoon, loading it with a spiced fish dish. She held it up to Vordan's lips to try.

"What are the rules of this Suthakar?" He accepted a taste of the offered fish, screwing up his face at the bitter flavors. Lenora smiled and ate the rest.

"It is a timed contest. It is not usually to the death. The fighters compete for twenty minutes, until one of them cannot continue, usually until one or the other is unconscious. A fighter may bow out early and accept defeat, but they will never be accepted into the clan, and will never be allowed to retry. If the twenty minutes finish and both participants are still fighting, then the challenger is accepted. The only other rule is against bringing other weapons into the fight."

"Can I use my claws?"

"Yes, it is part of you, as are his strength and size."

Dutak stood. "It is time for Suthakar."

Vordan hurriedly stood. "Is there anything else I should know?"

"You can only wear light pants and a shirt. No armor of any kind."

He nodded. Lenora towed him through the room to a door on the far side. It was open to reveal a round pit, several lengths across, lowered the height of a person into the ground. All around the pit was a gantry where people could watch the combat. There was no cover, no opportunity to hide or escape. He turned to her. "Your people do this so often, you have a purpose-built room for it?"

She shrugged helplessly. "Intergalactic crime clan, remember? Blood sports is a casual rest day activity."

He divested himself of his jacket, leaving just his loose black pants and shirt. After consideration, he dropped the shirt as well. Lenora sucked in a breath at the sight of him, chiseled muscles in pale skin. "Showing off much?"

"The shirt is too loose. Don't want to give him a grappling hold."

Lenora walked him up to an opening in the gantry. Gruarg was at an opening on the opposite side, her father standing next to him.

"Melee weapons are chosen for this Suthakar. Pick your weapon from the selection, challenger."

The crowd split to reveal a wall of weapons. Vordan examined them carefully, finally selecting a type of spear with a long curving blade on one end and a short sword blade on the other. It had detailed filigree up and down the shaft in a distinctive gold metal pattern.

"Pick your weapon from the selection, defender." Gruarg selected a large double handed axe/hammer.

"Enter the pit." Dutak's voice boomed through the chamber.

Both warriors jumped down the small drop onto the sand. Vordan took a couple of experimental swings with his spear, testing its weight and balance.

"Set timer. Twenty minutes, or until a challenger cannot continue. Challenger may quit at any time."

Two loud klaxons sounded, followed by a third longer, and a large timer was projected on the walls around the pit. It started counting down.

Vordan remained still, waiting. Gruarg stood, poised, waiting for him to attack, his axe/hammer held upright. When no attack was forthcoming, he roared at Vordan. "Are you afraid, little cat? Afraid to attack?"

Vordan smiled arrogantly. "It's called strategy. You might try it sometime. But then, perhaps not. It may be beyond you - I'm surprised you can actually speak at all."

Gruarg roared and swung at him. Vordan elegantly ducked under and swung his spear around in a whirling move that delivered double slices against Gruarg's hands where his fingers gripped the axe shaft. They exchanged places, pacing around the ring, each getting the measure of the other's speed. Vordan examined the other's hands where he had struck. As Lenora had indicated, there wasn't even a scratch. The skin was impenetrable to bladed weapons.

Gruarg swung again, this time much faster. Vordan ducked the first swing but was caught in an unexpected backswing, which smashed into his ribs and threw him across the pit to smash into the opposite wall. He climbed to his feet gingerly. It had been a glancing blow across the ribs from the hammer edge, leaving a long trailing cut that bled red blood. He probed it. At least two broken ribs. Judging his effectiveness compromised, but not critically so, he returned his attention to the Warrior. Clearly, Gruarg had been hiding his strength and speed. Grudgingly, Vordan reassessed his opponent.

The crowd cheered, some jeering at Lenora. He saw her out of the corner of her eye, unbothered by the display. She could have been waiting for an appointment. She gave every impression that she was supremely confident, that this was merely an inconvenient delay in their dinner plans.

Vordan considered the male. The skin could not be pierced, but perhaps there were softer parts. He raised his spear, feeling along the filigree for the telltale thin line. Locating it, he pressed and twisted just so, and the spear split into two, leaving him with a short-bladed sword and long-bladed scythe. The crowd oohed at the move. He had been delighted when he had spotted the distinctive Galatean pike in the weapons mix–it was a sparring favorite.

Considering his options, he feinted towards Gruarg, who raised his axe to defend on the right. Instead, Vordan spun left, running along the side of the pit and up the wall to land behind the hulking male. He swiped at the male's knees from behind with the scythe. He couldn't cut the skin, but a hit to the back of the knee would still off-balance an opponent–armored skin still responded to physics. Gruarg stumbled, going down onto one knee. Vordan stepped forward on the lower side, grabbed the male's head, pulled it back and shoved the short-bladed sword into his left eye.

As he did, he hit some sort of bone plate. He couldn't thrust it in fully to complete the kill, but he had accomplished one goal–the creature was now blind in one eye. He pulled the sword back and danced away, as Gruarg screamed in pain and dropped his axe to cover his wounded eye.

Vordan moved to the left, staying in his blind spot as Gruarg lumbered right, trying to keep him in sight. The crowd was totally silent, stunned at the unexpected turn of events. Gruarg groped for his axe again and swung, but his depth perception and aim were off. Vordan ducked under the axe and lightly danced out of the way. Gruarg bellowed at him, rage contorting his remaining features.

The time on the clock had not yet ticked over one minute. Vordan feinted again, jabbing at Gruarg with his scythe and short blade, forcing the male to spin around to see him, to slash out wildly. Vordan grinned fiercely, waiting for his opportunity. When he saw it, he took it. Gruarg swung wide right, and he simply stepped into the larger male's open arms and sliced at his right eye. He didn't stab this time, just sliced across, but it was enough. Gruarg dropped his axe and shrieked in agony. By luck, he caught Vordan across the face in his panicked motions, and Vordan was thrown across the pit to lie stunned against the wall.

He lay there for a few seconds, winded, listening to the creature shriek in pain. The faces of the Oonaugh showed their stark disbelief. They were absolutely silent. The timer clicked over two minutes.

Vordan stood slowly. "Dutak Oonaugh. Your champion is down, gravely wounded. If you end this now, you can still save his life and his sight. I can sit in this pit for another eighteen minutes, if required, to fulfill your traditions, while you all watch your companion die for the sake of your own pride. Is your pride worth his life?" Dutak remained silent, his face furious. "Is this what the clan is worth to you? I would never leave my clan brother that had fought for our honor, brought so low, for the sake of tradition and pride."

Vordan sat cross legged on the ground, stained with Gruarg's green blood, and waited.

The room was silent, everyone looking at Dutak, looking into the pit.

Finally, Dutak ground out. "It is done. Suthakar is satisfied. The mate of our daughter is worthy. Medics, assist our injured clan brother." He turned away in dismissal.

Sighing, Vordan stood, his injuries screaming at him. He kept his face blank, displaying no sign of the pain he was in. The other male had hit like a battering ram. He could feel bruises appearing all over him. The right side of his jaw felt like it was on fire after that last blow.

Lenora reached down into the pit and held out her hand, and he gratefully accepted her help in climbing back out. "Come this way. There is a room for us." She led him into a small chamber off the pit room which held a shower cubicle and a medic. He allowed himself to be cleaned up, and some topical medication applied to the cut on his ribs, as well as a painkiller.

Lenora was silent, waiting until the medic had left. Every touch, every bruise that was revealed as he cleaned off the sand and the sweat and the blood caused her frown to deepen, her jaw to tighten. Eventually, they stood in the room alone. The atmosphere was thick with unspoken words.

Casting around for the right thing to say, Vordan ventured, "I am alright, lady. You need not worry for my safety." Lenora opened her mouth to speak, then shook her head and thought better of it. "Verit are built for this. Literally genetically designed to take the punishment of battle and keep going. By tomorrow, I will be mostly healed."

"He could have killed you, Vordan," she hissed, fury and concern warring in her face.

"No, he couldn't have. That was theater, plain and simple. If I truly felt myself in danger, I would have got out of that pit and grabbed one of the security personnel's guns and shot him. We could have dealt with the fall out. All of this was because I was trying to adhere to your family's traditions."

"You think that makes it better? Knowing that you only got hurt because of my family and this ruse? You think that makes me feel any better about all of this?" Her anger broke. "You are my responsibility here. I got you into this. How do you think I felt, watching you being battered by Gruarg? I've seen him literally beat people into pulp dozens of times!"

His response was gentle, implacable. "I am my own responsibility, lady. Not yours. I accepted this mission, same as you, and I will do whatever is necessary to see to its success. Don't take on the responsibility for the world, Lenora. This isn't your fault or your call. I could have walked away at any time."

"That's where you are wrong, Vordan. This mission is mine to command, and you are here on my orders."

His own anger rose to meet hers. "I am a soldier, not a slave. Don't make the same mistake as the Maman and confuse the two!"

She stepped back, hurt. "How could you think I would see you as a slave, Vordan? Do you think so little of me?"

He was truly furious now. "How in the Goddess's name should I know what you think? You are a chameleon, lady. I guess you did inherit something from your reptile father. You change personality and story as easily as others change their clothes. I don't know if I've even met the real Lenorielle yet. At least what I do is honest. I fight and bleed for those I care about."

She looked as if he had struck her. Instantly, he regretted his harsh words. Before he could take them back, apologize, she spoke over him. "This has nothing to do with you being Verit. My team are all my responsibility." She shook her head to forestall any more comments. "I can't do this with you just now, Warrior. I must go and negotiate the deal with my family. I will see you back in the red wing. I'm sure you can make your own way there."

She was gone. The emptiness in the room made his own stupidity all the more obvious. He had lashed out at her, projecting his history with the Maman onto her. Anger and hurt together could only lead to one outcome. He sighed and pulled his clothing back on. He would see what he could do to repair the damage in the morning.

***

Lenora walked towards her father's office, shoving her fiery anger and pain down. She couldn't deal with it just now. Her father had summoned her, and to negotiate with Dutak, she would need all her wits about her. She knew the summons now was a tactic, as much as anything else. He was hoping that she would be emotionally unbalanced, and it would compromise her negotiation skills.

Unlike the grandeur of the temple, Dutak's office was small and cluttered. It had always been that way, the shelves lining it filled with trinkets and trophies from his travels. Her father sat behind his desk, her Melati on a comfortable divan next to a small fire, her feet up on a stool. Her sister Ari was nowhere in sight.

"Come in, Elle. We have much to discuss." Her father beckoned her to sit in a chair across the desk from him. They sat, looking at each other in the dim light. "It is good to see you, Daughter. You look well."

She nodded. "And you too, Father."

"We missed you. When I had heard you had gone to join your mother, I thought it was a visit. That you would become bored with her quiet life and return to us. Then, when we heard you had joined the military... I thought you lost to us forever. Yet here you are, back in the home of the Oonaugh once more." He grinned. "And with a Verit mate, no less. I would expect nothing less of my daughter. He is impressive, a fitting match for you."

She nodded again, remaining silent.

"Tell us then, what deal you offer? I know you well enough that you have not come back to rejoin us."

She took a deep breath. "Do I have your word that you will keep this secret, whatever you decide about the deal?"

Her father pondered, the firelight reflecting off his scales. "I do."

"I am hunting someone. Someone has been attacking my new home world, hiring mercs. I want to know who."

"What is it you think I can help with?"

"I want the name of the person that hired the mercs that attacked Dalat colony last month. They came on an Alliance ship."

Her father whistled. "These are dangerous waters, Daughter. Big players."

"Then you know who it is?"

"Of course, I do. My daughter lives in the colony. Do you think I wouldn't know what was going on there?"

She nodded. He was right. Whatever his faults, her father had been deeply protective of his children. No insult had ever gone unrepaid.

"What do you offer?"

"Five micrograms of Zyilan."

He stilled. "You want this information that much?"

"We do. They came to my home, Father. Tried to take what was ours. I will find them and punish them." She was surprised at the viciousness in her own voice, how much she meant it.

He grinned widely. "There you are, my Lenorielle. I had hoped you had not lost your fire, submerged in your mother's soft people." He looked over at Melati, silently communicating. "We will give you this information. On one condition."

"What is that?"

"You will come and visit us again. We all miss you. We accept your life choices, but we cannot accept your absence from our lives. Family is all we have."

Lenora's breath caught in her throat, ambushed by surprise at the surge of emotion. She swallowed and licked her lips, responding huskily, "I agree. Thank you."

Her father blinked, connecting his HUD to hers. When she accepted the connection, the information she needed floated to her. There it was, the codename of the buyer "MUSHIT." It meant nothing to her.

"You should know, word is that they will have another job on the market soon. A stop and seize for a logistics route." He smiled at her. "Should be something you'd excel at, Daughter."

She removed the plain, unmarked canister of Zyilan from inside her shirt and handed it over to him.

His eyes widened in surprise as he accepted its slight weight. "Where did it come from?"

"That's classified, Father. It's real. That's all you need to know."

He examined her closely, squinting, trying to read her. She gave nothing away, impassive. All Alliance canisters were sold in Alliance branded vessels, where you could track the sale back to its original mining source. The plain canister screamed it was unofficial.

"If you have an alternative source of Zyilan, let me know. There are lots of aliens willing to trade for it. It would be very lucrative." She said nothing. She could give nothing away. This was what her father did best, ferret out secrets. It was his greatest skill; one he had passed down to her. "Lots of us are sick of the Alliance and its humans-first approach. Think about it. It's a big universe outside the human colonies."

"Thank you, Father. If it's alright, I'll go now and leave you."

"Do you have to, child?" Melati asked. "I had hoped, now that business is done, you would sit with me a while."

Lenora laughed. "You mean let you ply me with alcohol and questions until you pry my secrets out of me?"

Melati smiled enigmatically. "I have missed you, Elle."

"And I you. I would be honored to sit by the fire with you."

"And a few drinks?" her father asked.

She laughed again. "A couple of drinks."

She dragged her chair over to the fire and got comfortable as her father ordered the drinks. Just for a while, for a few hours at least, she could be just Elle again. Here, with her father and Melati. It warmed parts of her soul that she hadn't even realized had gone cold.

Chapter Eight

Pull a Thread

The next morning, Lenora comm'd Zera on her HUD as she stuffed her belongings back into her pack, urgency thrumming in her veins.

Zera answered on the first call. "What's up, Elle?" she chirped.

"We have a lead. We have the name of the merc that hired the team, and he has another contract out just now. We are going to take it."

Zera whooped in response.

"What's happening?" came a voice from offscreen of the HUD, and Zera turned to repeat what she had told her. She heard a male voice cheer in response.

"Odran says congratulations too."

"We need to show some muscle when we bid. My sister will loan me a few personnel, but I need more warriors."

Zera frowned. "I can ask the Dagger Kiss if they'll loan us some, but they are an elite unit. They don't have those types of numbers."

Odran spoke again from offscreen, and this time it was muffled. Zera rolled her eyes in aggravation. "Give me a minute." Zera put her on hold. Lenora raced around her room, grabbing the rest of her things while she waited and moved back int the lounge room, where she met Vordan who was doing the same.

"Ready?" he asked.

"Yeah, just updating Zera."

Zera came back into view. "Odran has an idea. I'm going to add him to the comm." Odran appeared in a window next to Zera. "He says that we should ask the Maman for some Verit warriors. They are mercs, after all, and a combined force of Verit, Falosian, and Oonaugh should be mixed enough not to attract attention."

Lenora considered. "It's a good idea, but it can't be Dathalka. Everyone knows that the Dathalka clan runs the colony—we may as well put up a sign that says, 'spies are here.'"

Vordan motioned to her, and she added him, too. "What about Tothas? I still have contact with my old clan, and they are well known."

They considered. "We'd still need the request to go from the Maman."

Zera smiled at her. "Fortunately, we have a Maman on board."

"You're not serious!" responded Lenora. "Scara is green as Earth grass. She's just turned sixteen. They'll never listen to her."

Vordan squirmed. "Actually, they will. Maman-La are given to other clans to raise, and to widen the gene pool. But Scara was born Tothas. The Maman in charge of the clan is her mother."

There was a long pause before Zera laughed. "Well, I guess that's handy."

Lenora nodded once. "Alright, let's do it. Zera, discuss with Scara and make the call to both the Tothas and the Dagger Kiss. We will make ourselves known to the buyer and bid for the contract. I'll let you know when we have the details."

"Yes, ma'am. Acknowledged," confirmed Zera.

They signed off and Lenora turned to look at Vordan. The tension from last night lay between them. She wasn't sure how to pierce it when he stepped forward and took her hands. "I'm sorry, Lenora. For what I said last night. I was angry and lashed out. I didn't mean to hurt you."

She was taken aback. In her experience, males rarely apologized. "I am sorry as well. I didn't mean to imply you were lesser. But this mission is under my command. You are all my responsibility."

He nodded. "I understand. I won't let it get in the way again."

She stood back and plastered a smile on her face to hide her lingering confusion. There were too many things unsaid between them, this strange intimacy that the past two days had created warring with this polite distance.

Lenora grabbed the little knife and wire that were sitting next to her pack. "Thank you for the loan."

He looked at them, then pushed them back to her. "No, keep them. They suit you."

It was unexpected, like so many things about him. She had no idea how to respond. Like she always did when emotions got complicated, she focused on her work. She thrust them back into her pack. She turned back and examined him critically, noting that his wounds were already well on their way to healing, the more minor ones already nothing but faint red lines. "How functional are you?"

He grinned at the innuendo, at her blatant attempt to change the subject and keep a distance between them, but resisted the urge to needle her. "I am eighty percent functional and will be back to full operating efficiency by this evening. Cuts, bruises, and soft tissue damage are easy for a Verit to heal."

She nodded, her eyes tracing the remains of a deep cut on the side of his face. "Good." She paused. She couldn't leave it like this. Whatever her feelings, he had placed himself in danger for her, and tried to set things to right between them. She had to show the same courage.

She took a tentative step towards him, placing a hand on his chest. "Thank you, Vordan, for everything. I couldn't have done this without you."

He smiled and placed his hand over hers. "It was my pleasure, lady. Your wish is my command, as the Goddess wills it." Their eyes connected, and she felt the moment of searing intimacy down to her bones. This wasn't the cocky flyboy, or the angry, competent warrior, or the teasing friend... this was something else entirely. Something dark, glittering with promise.

She licked her dry lips. "Is that so?"

His eyes tightened, awareness electric between them. "It is."

She tilted her head up towards him. "And what if it wasn't a command? If you had a choice? What would you do then?" she whispered.

He leaned in, his cheek against hers, his lips on her ears. "Are you sure you want to know the answer to that?"

She nodded. One hand gripped the back of her neck, his thumb under her jaw, tilting her face away from him. The other hand trailed up her side, skirting the curve of her breast to her shoulder. He nuzzled the mass of her hair back to expose her nape and bent over, setting his teeth to her in blatant possession. She shuddered in response, her hands gripping his shoulders, flexing, unsure if she wanted to haul him closer or push him away. He nipped at her nape, tiny bites punctuated by little kisses as he worked his way up to her cheekbone to feather kisses to the corner of her mouth. He licked the seam of her lips, probing for entry, before he swept in and consumed her. He held her tightly as he deepened the kiss, and she moaned in response as they went up in flames.

It was incredible, unlike anything she had ever experienced before. She had mated in the past, but this... his long drugging kisses were flat out the hottest she had ever experienced. Eventually, he gentled the kiss, breathing heavily. He pressed his forehead to hers, nuzzling her. "I would do all sorts of wicked things, my lady. You need only signal your interest."

She breathed heavily, desperately trying to get control of her raging hormones. "Holy shit," she replied weakly, and he grinned in response, all proud arrogance. "You are a dangerous male, Vordan." Bastard knew exactly what he had done to her.

She shuddered and stepped back, feeling strangely light. "I see. Well, then." She turned and grabbed her pack and sauntered to the doorway. She felt his eyes on her the entire way, and she had never felt sexier. "We will have to explore further. When we have more time."

He nodded slowly in response, his grin wolfish. "When we have more time."

They exited into the garden and met Ari at the red wing entrance. Ari embraced her, squeezing her tight. "I'm glad I got to see you, even if it was for Falosian business. Don't be a stranger, Elle. I miss you."

She returned the squeeze, her eyes misting. "I miss you too. When this is over, come visit us at the new colony."

Ari stepped back, dashing tears away from her jewel-colored eyes. "Alright, enough emotions for now." She raised her arm and pressed a section of her metal cuff. "Father has briefed me on the deal. I've sent you the last known address of the buyer."

"What is his name?" asked Vordan. Ari grimaced.

"He's a bug."

Vordan paused. "I don't understand the significance."

"His species is insectoid. Their language doesn't really translate. We don't even have a good name for the species, we just call them bugs."

"What do you call him then?"

Ari shrugged. "The buyer. He is the go-between for all major merc deals on Rilaz. His people have a compound in the gamma sector. You need to go through him to bid on the job."

Lenora groaned. "The gamma sector?"

Ari smiled sympathetically. "Sorry. But it's the only way to get to him."

"What's wrong with the gamma sector?"

"It's one of the few places on Rilaz where Oonaugh doesn't have control. It's pretty far out of the city, in the closet thing we have to urban sprawl, and it's run by clan Vicious Crow."

Vordan was skeptical. "Vicious Crow? Are they a group of twelve-year-olds?"

"Unfortunately, not. They are strong, fast, and vicious. They are all male, and don't have the best reputation with females. Gamma sector is not a safe place for females to go. The only good thing is that they aren't the brightest–they mostly stick to drugs, alcohol, and other intoxicants. They produce and black-market."

"And?" prompted Ari, making big eyes at her sister.

Lenora squirmed, her gaze everywhere but at Vordan. "And their leader is Trent Elder. We used to have a thing."

Vordan stared at her for a long minute before guffawing. "You used to date the leader of some hick moonshine gang with the name of a bad emo band?"

Lenora sighed. "It's not like that. I was infiltrating the alcohol trade. We wanted one of the contracts they had, so I seduced my way in. I thought we were both using each other–he was using me as a way into the Oonaugh clan, and I was stealing his contacts. I didn't realize until too late that he meant it - he really had feelings. I had to end it, and he didn't take it well."

"Oh, this gets better and better. We are going into alien hillbilly country where your jilted ex emo-moonshine-gang-leader lover will shoot us on sight, to find a mysterious mercenary go-between gray market auctioneer, to somehow try and bid for a contract to undertake some nefarious action on the bare hope that we will trace it back to someone higher in their organization that might know something about whoever attacked the colony."

"Yes."

"Just making sure I understand it."

"Yes." She bared her teeth. "If you want to bail, feel free to leave. You know where the door is."

He laughed out loud. "Are you kidding? This is insane and hasn't a hope of succeeding, but it's the most fun I've had in years. Lead on, my queen."

Lenora was nonplussed and Ari laughed, clapping her hands. "Oh, Elle, I really like this one. I hope you keep him." She turned and motioned for them to follow them. "Come on, I'll take you back to your shuttle."

Chapter Nine

Gamma Sector

G amma sector looked like the physical personification of the-morning-after-the-night-before. It was gray, dirty, and everything was slightly non-functional.

They landed on a shuttle pad, amongst more than a dozen other beat-up shuttles. Vordan looked mournfully at the shining shuttle as they left it, sticking out like a sore thumb. "Will it still have its taillights and fins when we get back?"

Lenora patted him on the shoulder in commiseration. "Not a chance, buddy."

They were swathed in long, dark gray cloaks from head to toe, each of them bristling with weapons. Vordan had resisted initially, but as they merged into the crowd, he had to admit that she had been correct. Nearly everyone they saw, regardless of species, was wrapped in a cloak of some variety. People peered out of hard eyes as they passed, assessing them as both predator and prey. "How can people live like this?" he murmured sub-vocally, their HUDs connected to each other to form a private comms channel.

Lenora shrugged. "Some have no choice. For others, their situation is complex and multi-faceted, a web of addiction and abuse. There isn't much in the way of social services in places like Rilaz, and certainly not out here on the fringe. Most of the charities and shelters will only take people if they are clean and sober. The drug addiction houses won't take people with violent crime backgrounds... so on and so on. Others choose to be here, to live in the gray, for their own reasons."

Vordan's face was flat, showing no emotions. "The clan structures on Verit are so restrictive and borderline abusive... but at least we look after everyone. None of our brothers would be allowed to fall so low."

"Do you really think so? I wonder. Every society has those that fall behind. That cannot function in the mold that society requires of them. If you don't see them in yours, I wonder where they go."

Vordan didn't respond. They walked on, past dilapidated shops with grimy windows. Alien electric music blared from the occasional open door of bars they passed. Eventually, they came to an open square where a market was in full swing. All around, stalls sold food, clothing, second hand electronics, potions, medications ... a mishmash of items. Lenora checked her HUD. "Apparently, the buyer has a comms repair shop somewhere in this square, next to a food stall."

"Alright, let's split up. Message when you find it."

Lenora nodded in agreement and moved left to start working her way around the market perimeter. Vordan turned right, edging around a mother and her children haggling over food. He tried his best to hold his breath. The scents of the unwashed assaulted his sensitive feline senses.

The hairs on the back of his neck prickled, and he turned slightly, under the guise of examining an ancient blaster in a weapons stall, noting the male following him. He continued on, spotting a second small male darting between two stalls and pacing him on the other side. Gauging their worn clothing, the hard hungry look in their eyes and their youth, he figured them for thieves rather than gang members.

He turned down an aisle into a quieter avenue and paused to examine some jewelry. Out of the corner of his eye, he watched the males signal to each other before one made his way clumsily down the aisle towards him while the other moved out of sight.

When the clumsy male was near him, he stumbled into him. Vordan twisted around in a lightning-fast move and gripped the clumsy male by the back of the neck and tossed him at the second male, who had appeared from the shadows between two stalls, clearly intending to take advantage of his distraction. The males tumbled in a tangle of arms and legs, and Vordan was on them.

He slapped one across the face with just enough strength to stun, and hauled the other upright by his neck, bringing the scrawny male up to his face.

On closer inspection, Vordan realized they were much younger than he had initially thought, barely into their teens. The grime and hard-eyed looks had hidden much, and the one he now held scrabbled ineffectually at his gauntleted arm in an attempt to release himself.

"I don't like being robbed," he offered conversationally. "And I would hang up my furs in shame if I let myself be robbed by two children. Where are your parents? Do you not have elders that should care for you?"

"Let him go!" screeched the one on the floor in a high-pitched voice as he attempted to get to his feet, and Vordan looked down in shock.

"Look at me!" commanded Vordan, and the one on the floor glared at him, spitting fire with his eyes. *Her* eyes, Vordan realized. The smaller one was female, and young. Vordan was swamped with guilt when he realized he had hit a female. Never in his life had he raised his hand to that gender. It violated everything he believed in, an affront to the goddess.

Vordan dropped the male he was holding, who collapsed to the ground gasping for breath. He crouched down and reached for the female, cursing aloud when she shied away, fear clouding her eyes.

"It is alright, lady. I won't harm you. I would not have hit you, had I realized."

For some reason, this froze her up in fear more. "I ain't no female!" her voice quavered. "You got it wrong. Just let us go, we didn't take nothin'." Her little chin tipped up in anger, wobbling slightly in her fear.

"I ask you again, little one. Where are your elders? Who should be caring for you?"

She shrugged defensively. "Got no one. No dad. Mama died two years ago. Just me and Lett now. We do alright."

"Is there no organization that would take you in? That you need not do this?"

The boy coughed behind him. "The sisters of divine light feed us, sometimes. No one else but the crows."

"Ah, this gang I have heard of."

The girl blanched. "Can't go near the crows."

The boy crawled over to her, wrapping a skinny arm around her skinnier shoulder. "Crows ain't a good place to be a girl, less you want to whore."

Vordan's heart sank at the casualness that they spoke of their circumstances. They sat in awkward silence for a moment as he racked his brain on how he could help them. "Can we go, mister?" she asked quietly.

Vordan considered them. He couldn't just leave like this. He owed the little female a debt for harming her. "Well, my companion and I are looking for someone. If you tell me where they are, I will give you five credits."

"Ten," she promptly replied, and he resisted the urge to laugh.

"Five. And I will buy you dinner of your choosing from any stall in this market."

They looked at each other before the female responded. "Fine, food first. No funny stuff."

As she looked at him, with her too wise young eyes, his heart sank. "Little one, I know you don't know me, but I am of Verit. My name is Vordan of Clans Dathalka and Tothas. We do not harm females."

She looked at him skeptically. "You hit me."

He grimaced. "In my defense, you were trying to rob me, and were dressed as a male."

She considered. "Alright. Who are you looking for?"

"A bug that runs a comms shop in this square. Next to a food stall of some kind."

They exchanged glances. "We know him," the male responded eventually.

"Then lead on, lady. Where would you like to eat?"

She led him through several aisles to a busy stall, redolent with the smells of meat and bread. They waited in the line until they reached the front, where, with quicksilver glances at him, she ordered two skewers and a loaf of bread. When it arrived, it was pitifully small.

"Is that it?" he asked her, and she cocked an eyebrow at him, considering. After a long moment, she grinned, and ordered several more loaves and several slices of roast. He remained silent, paying when asked, and watched them eat only the smallest portion.

Assessing their consumption, he suspected he had just bought them enough food for several days. When they had their fill, they looked at him expectantly.

"I have met your first term. Now, where is the bug?"

They led him just a few aisles away, to a prosperous looking shop with a real glass window filled with comms equipment and components. There was no text, but a large carved sign hung over the door with what looked like a stylized prawn.

He looked down at his small guides. "Thank you." He fished out the credits and handed them over, and they promptly vanished into various pockets like magic.

The male looked at him seriously. "If you survive the buyer, and need another guide, ask anywhere for Lett or Shari. We'll guide you again."

"How did you know that I'm looking for the buyer?"

Shari snorted. "Big outsider with weapons and good boots? Only one reason your kind visits the bug."

She was so smart. He couldn't just leave them. It would haunt him for the rest of his days. He crouched down again. "I know you don't know me, and have no reason to trust me, but hear me when I say that this isn't the only life available. If you want out of here, I will give you a lift to wherever you want to go. My shuttle is on pad three at the landing bay. When my business is done, meet me there, and I'll take you."

Shari shrank back. "Do you think we're stupid? That we'd just go with some male in a shuttle?"

"I have a female companion with me. She'll vouch for me."

Shari shuddered. "Females are just as bad sometimes."

He considered his next move, praying to the Goddess that he wasn't making a mistake. "I will tell you who she is, but you must keep it a secret. She is Lenorielle of the Oonaugh."

Shari's eyes went wide as dinner plates. "Elle! The Black Valkyrie," she breathed in awe. "But I heard she disappeared!"

"She was working a job. Now she's back."

Shari and the boy looked at each other again in silent communication. "You've dealt well with us, so fair's fair. You should know that there's a bounty out on her in the gamma sector. The Crows."

He nodded. "We'll keep a low profile. But if you want out, she'll vouch for me."

Shari was stubborn. She gave no sign of her interest. "We'll think about it."

Vordan stood and nodded. He could do no more. He had given them the choice; it was more than most would get. "I expect I'll be an hour or so. Think fast."

He turned and moved towards the store, comming Lenora on the HUD as he did. "I've found the shop. I'm going in."

"Dammit, Vordan, wait for me."

"I think I can manage this, Lenora. I'm just asking to speak to the buyer."

Vordan ducked into the shop, finding himself in an open area facing a streamlined metal counter, the walls full of racks of comms equipment behind metal security cage covers.

The bug sat behind the counter. Sitting down, it was slightly taller than Vordan, swathed in a dark cloak, so that only its head was showing. Its head was oval, with layers of shiny green chitin. It had large, black, faceted eyes and multi-jointed, mandible jaws. The bug buzzed, the sound making Vordan's teeth ache slightly, and from a box on the counter a computer voice spoke. "Welcome to Bug's. How can I help you today?"

Vordan approached the counter. "I am looking for someone."

"This is a comm shop. We don't do information," came the computer-generated voice again, after a slight delay.

"I need to speak to the buyer."

The cloak rustled, and Vordan realized it wasn't fabric, it was wings wrapped around the creature. "I don't know who that is. If you don't wish to purchase comms equipment, please leave."

"Please don't do this. This doesn't have to be hard. I represent a group interested in bidding for work. We have impeccable references, and you will find us highly competitive."

There was a longer pause this time. "Who sent you?"

"I represent Elle of the Oonaugh."

"She's dead." The reply was immediate, the dead artificial voice somehow conveying scorn.

"No, she isn't. She was working a job, and she's back now. We would like to speak to the buyer." Vordan remained calm, but as the conversation continued, his senses were screaming at him that danger was increasing, and the damned buzzing was making his teeth ache more with each second.

"The buyer does not wish to speak to you."

"Can you check, please? I'm happy to wait."

"I have checked. The buyer does not wish to speak to you."

Vordan shrugged off his cloak, revealing his body suit and armor. He rested his hand on his sword. "I'm afraid I will have to insist on discussing the matter with the buyer myself."

***

A creature shrieked. A long, undulating, wailing cry that raised the hairs on Lenora's arms. She raced through the market, dodging people and stalls, blades up. When she reached the corner where the shop was, she skid to a stop, her mouth gaping in shock. Vordan stumbled backwards out of a doorway, crashing into a market stall. The stallholder puffed up its feathers and squawked at him in anger, shoving him off with a tirade of screeching curses punctuated with thrown vegetables.

Vordan landed on his ass on the tiled walkway in the piazza, covered head to toe in green goop. Out of the doorway emerged a giant insectoid. Its legs emerged first, green chitin shimmering with red highlights as they unfolded. Its upper body reared back, revealing a dark red maw rimmed in sharp chitinous ridges, dripping more of the green goo.

"Need help, Flyboy?" she called as she started wading through the tide of shoppers frantically trying to get out of the fight zone.

He laughed. The idiot *laughed*. "No, your ladyship. I'll be right there." He flipped backwards into a crouch and trained a gun on the creature. She blinked. Where *in the Goddess' name did he pull that from?*

He shot the creature's right foreleg, and it wailed again. Lenora clenched her teeth against the pain as the sound crescendoed, vibrating through her bones and making her teeth rattle. The remaining patrons in the market scattered.

Vordan snarled at it. "Now, tell me where the buyer is."

It hissed at him, shooting another gob of goo at his feet, and swiping with a ridged foreleg. He ducked and shot the offending limb. "I'm afraid that I don't have all day. I'm on a schedule. The only question is whether you run out of legs before I get my answers."

"Vordan, stop!" she shouted, but she was drowned out by the crowd's noise as she struggled to get to him.

The creature shuddered and began shaking from the depths of its body still hidden within the building, to the tip of its antennae, the motions becoming increasingly more frantic until it was battering itself against the sides of the open doorway. It stopped, frozen still, and Lenora noticed a new sound. It was pitched low, rumbling, and she felt it as a pressure against her ears. The creature froze for a long moment before its head disintegrated. It burst in a flood of green goo and goblets, the flesh sagging. From within emerged dozens of smaller versions, with tiny iridescent wings. The creatures swarmed Vordan, and he went down under the weight of their bodies.

"Oh, for the love of the Goddess!" she cursed. She strode into the foray, gripping the creatures and tossing them off Vordan to reveal him covered in tiny bites. She hauled him to his feet. "Why are you asking it where the buyer is?" she yelled.

He wobbled and looked at her funny. "Because we need to find the buyer?"

"That is the buyer." She pointed at the swarm and the decaying body. "They are a hive mind. They are all the buyer, you idiot! This is why I told you to wait for me. You have no idea what you are doing! Plus, you got hurt. Again!"

He looked down at himself. "It's only minor. It'll heal in moments."

"No, it won't. The pupa form is highly toxic. You'll need anti-venin immediately."

Lenora turned to the bugs that were flitting around in a frenzy. She accessed her HUD and broadcast a broad-range, high-pitched signal. Immediately, the creatures slowed, then stopped moving altogether. They drooped to the floor, settling into heaps, their wings gently fluttering.

"Did you kill them?" Vordan asked.

She cast him a slashing glance. "Of course not. I don't kill young of any species if I can avoid it. Especially when I'm trying to make a deal with them." She looked around the now empty market and saw a basket weaver stall nearby. Grabbing a discarded basket, she scooped up one of the creatures.

"So you won't kill young, but you'll kidnap?" he quipped, feeling suddenly lightheaded.

She didn't respond, just glared at him as she stomped into the wreckage of the shop front. She moved to the counter, which by some miracle of the goddess was still standing, and grabbed the silver translation box.

He continued on, "I just want to make sure I know where your boundaries are. For future reference." As he spoke, he wobbled again, his legs going weak suddenly. He sat down abruptly on the debris covered ground.

Fastening the small basket with the creature inside it to her belt, Lenora rushed to his side. "We need to get you anti-venin. Their venom is lethal, and you've got dozens of bites." She felt for his pulse, feeling the racing pulsing under her fingertips. She pulled his arm over her shoulder and hauled him up. "On your feet, WARRIOR!" she commanded.

Lenora was tall for a female, but he towered over her. He was surprisingly heavy, even for his size, as if his bones were denser than expected. They drunkenly lurched towards the market entrance when Lenora pulled them to a stop. Ahead, she saw a slim figure picking through the debris left by the market exodus. Steadying Vordan with one hand, she pulled her gun with the other.

"Either fight or leave. I don't have time for this," she called. After a few seconds, the figure detached from the shadows and moved to her, standing just outside of reach. She lowered her gun slightly, realizing that it was a child—a young male. She extended her empathic senses, feeling only wariness and... hope? How odd.

"Who are you? What do you want?" she asked.

"S'Lett," mumbled Vordan. She looked at the young male enquiringly.

"My name is Lett," he confirmed. "What happened to him?"

"He got bit by a pupa bug." Lett winced. "Do you know if there is a MedBay nearby?"

The boy shook his head. "No public MedBay in Gamma sector, but I know a healer that can help."

Yes, and she was born yesterday. "Ah ha, and I should just follow you. Why?"

Lett looked at her with that strange mix of wariness and hope again. "Because he fed us. He paid us. He said you'd help us escape."

"He did, did he?" she muttered, looking at Vordan. Vordan nodded, but even that seemed to exhaust him.

"Why?"

"Are you really Ella Oonaugh?" the boy asked.

Lenora sighed. "Yes, I'm Lenorielle Oonaugh."

The boy searched her face, gauging her sincerity. Evidently, whatever he saw there was enough. "My sister, Shari, she isn't safe here. We want passage out of the gamma sector. In exchange, we'll get you to a healer with anti-venin. You'll need to pay for it yourself." He waited for her to nod in agreement before he carried on. "We'll also guide you to your shuttle."

Lenora snorted. "I know where I parked my shuttle, young one."

He smiled tightly. "You've been spotted, lady. The crows are looking for you. You'll never get there without a firefight. Not without us."

She considered. Vordan was fading fast. They really didn't have a choice. "Deal. Lead us to the healer."

Lett turned to go, and she reached out with the butt of her gun to tap him on the shoulder. "But beware, children. If you betray us, I'll kill you myself." The young male gulped and nodded.

As they moved on, she heard Vordan murmur sub-vocally into her HUD. "No, you wouldn't. You don't kill young of any species."

"He doesn't need to know that," she replied and saw the barest hint of a grin on Vordan's face.

"Come on, Flyboy. Let's go. You weigh a ton. We need to put you on a diet."

He chuckled rustily, but she was alarmed to hear a slight wheeze in his lungs.

The boy led them through the township, picking his way from shadow to shadow until they arrived at a nondescript wooden door. There was no signage, nothing to show a healer was in residence. She propped Vordan up against a wall, her arms, legs and back burning and shaking with the stress of hauling him.

The boy knocked once and slipped inside. One minute turned into two as she stood guarding Vordan. Eventually, a withered old male appeared, blinking owlishly in the light. He eyed Vordan up and down, and asked in a heavy accent, "Species?"

"Verit. Human-template, feline hybrid," she replied.

"How long bitten?"

"Half an hour. Maybe more."

He grunted. "He might survive. Come in."

She pulled Vordan in, surprised to find the inside was a fully kitted MedBay, shining sterile white. It would not have been out of place on any Alliance planet. She deposited Vordan on a bed where the healer had motioned. "Credits or trade?" he asked again.

"Depends how much?"

The male looked at Vordan. "Big male, weighs much. Two vials. Three hundred credits."

Lett whistled low. Lenora didn't even blink. It was daylight robbery, but she didn't have time to waste haggling. "Done. Now heal him."

"Proof money first," the male replied, as he moved to a refrigeration unit in the corner and pulled out the vials.

Ha! And I have a seaside villa on Paradise to sell you, thought Lenora. "Half now, half later. If he lives."

The male scratched an eyebrow. "No guarantee life."

"Then no payment."

He grunted again. "Fine." He held up a hand and projected his credit codes. He must have had some sort of embedded AI within his palm. She transferred him the credits with her HUD.

He administered two pressure injectors, one to either side of Vordan's neck, and she winced at seeing the old-fashioned tech piercing his skin.

"What now?" she asked.

"Wait. Live no live. Up to him. Two, three hours. Know then."

"Thank you."

"No thanks. Payment." replied the elderly male, smiling widely to reveal gleaming white, sharpened teeth. "I work. Other patients. You wait here." He pulled over a seat next to Vordan's bed, then moved away and through another door, deeper into the building.

She sat for long moments, just watching his vitals on the machines. As she stilled, the focused efficiency that had filled her while they were looking for the healer drained away, leaving her hollow and scared. Stupid flyboy could have got himself killed. Why didn't he wait for her? He could have ruined the mission and *got himself killed*. For what? Arrogance? Proving a point? Urgh, she wanted him to get better so that she could kill him herself for making her so terrified.

It filled her with fear at how quick she had become used to him, to his stupid jokes and humor. The thought of continuing the mission without him... No. She wouldn't go there. Not even hypothetically. The healer's anti-venin would work. He was Verit. Their constitution was legendary. He would be fine. She'd wait until he was better, so that she could blister his skin with her lecture when he was well enough to hear and truly appreciate it.

That decided, she pushed all thoughts of fear or failure out of her mind. A motion in the corner of her eye caught her attention, and she realized that the young male was in the room with her.

"How did he help you?" she asked.

The little male shuffled. "We tried to rob him. He caught us, then fed us and paid us to guide him to the bug." He was quiet, his response whispered. "He was kind." The last was said with awe, as if the concept of kindness was so rare.

"He is kind," she agreed.

"I need to go. I need to get Shari. I'll bring her back here."

"Alright. We'll be here a couple of hours at least."

He nodded and slipped out, leaving her and Vordan alone in the silence of the clean MedBay. It was surreal after the chaos of the past hour. Eventually, she roused herself. She had to finish the mission.

She unclipped the cage from her belt and saw that the little creature was still asleep from the sound stun she had used. She took out the translation box, and connected it to her HUD, and re-synced it to the little creature.

Using a carefully modulated sound wave, she woke up the little creature. It promptly spat at her and rushed the bars of the little basket.

"Now, now, there's no need for that," she crooned. "Stop pretending, Buyer. I know who you are." The creature stilled. "Talk to me. I've sync'd the translation matrix for you."

"Release me at once," the creature spoke through the box.

"I will shortly. I have no desire to be bitten today. Let's have a little chat first."

"I will kill you and your family for this! You attacked my shop!"

"No, we didn't. We came to talk, to bid. The damage to your shop was entirely your own doing." It remained mutinously silent. "Besides, are you sure you want to take on the Oonaugh?"

The creature peered at her. "Who are you?" it demanded.

"I am Lenorielle Oonaugh."

"Impossible." The reply was immediate. "She's dead."

"No, I'm not. I was working at a job, and now I'm back. My father will vouch for my return if need be. I am starting a new venture. I've put together a little merc group. Some ships, a hundred or so troops. We want to bid for work."

The creature trilled. Whatever sentiment it was expressing, the translator couldn't interpret it. "You were never into merc work. You were an elegant artist, not a thug."

"This venture will be elegant. We will undertake precision strikes, undercover wet work. In five years, we'll be the go-to for elite mercs in the quadrant."

The creature considered. "Very well. The next auction is on Valhalla in one week. Usually, we would take remote or proxy bids, but as a new company, you must attend in person. Go to the Red Sea Casino, ask for the Ruby Room."

"Very well."

"Now release this one."

She grabbed the basket and took it outside. Carefully grabbing hold of the lid, she positioned herself to slam the door closed the second she opened the lid, just in case they were tempted to impart any last gifts. It was anti-climactic when the creature simply flew away into the dirty gray sky.

Breathing out a sigh of relief, she comm'd Zera, informing her they had the location of the merc auction, and that they were waiting for Vordan to recover from an injury, before heading their way.

"Do you need an evac?"

"No, we are alright for now. I'll let you know if anything changes."

"Remember, we're nearby."

Mission completed, she returned to her vigil at Vordan's bedside. When she sat down, she noticed that Vordan's eyes were open, and her heart sang. "Hey there Flyboy, how are you feeling?" She kept her voice steady, light, no hint of the emotion rushing through her.

"Like my shuttle fell on me," he croaked.

"You're lucky. Looks like we got the anti-venin in time."

He looked around. "Where is the kid?"

"Gone to find his sister."

"I heard what you did with the bug. You got the info, completed the mission." She nodded. "Thank you. I'm glad I didn't screw it up beyond all hope." He sighed.

"You did make a pretty big mess, Flyboy, but I figure we're even since you saved our butts in the Oonaugh contest." He smiled faintly. "Rest for a bit more. The healer said that it'll be a couple of hours before you're back on your feet. We won't be going anywhere until the kids get back." She stroked his iron hair back from his face. "I'll stand guard."

"Thank you, Pirate Queen." He closed his eyes, content that she would take care of everything.

***

Their respite was short-lived. Less than an hour later, the kids burst into the MedBay. A little girl slid to a stop next to the bed. "We have to go now. The Crows are coming."

Lenora nodded. "Healer!" she roared, and the male scuttled in. "We must leave immediately. Can he be moved?"

The Healer grabbed a tablet and activated the medical bed, displaying Vordan's vitals. "Yes, for a brief trip. Anti-venin worked. Need more rest. Ten to twelve hours."

"Thank you."

"Pay before go," the male stated firmly.

Lenora pulled up his details and transferred the remaining credits. "Done with my thanks."

"Don't get killed. Pay customers hard to find. You need a healer again, come to me. I fix." The male nodded his thanks and left.

Lenora helped Vordan get to his feet. He groaned but was at least able to keep himself upright. "I can move, but I'm less than twenty percent operational effectiveness in combat."

"It's alright, Flyboy, I've got this one."

"Lead on, Pirate Queen."

The kids watched them banter back and forth with eyes as wide as saucers.

"Lett, guide us. Take us to the shuttle."

Their diminutive guides let them out into the warren of the township again, sneaking through backyards of businesses and hiding in shadowed doorways. They made it all the way to the landing bay before they hit trouble. At the edge of the landing bay, Shari pulled them down to a crouch behind an ancient troop transport hover vehicle. They peered around the edge to see several guards stationed around their shuttle.

"Shit," Vordan mumbled, and Lenora nodded in agreement.

"Odds of winning in a fight?" she asked him, and he considered.

"Less than one in ten. I am at reduced capacity, and there is little cover. We only have you. Your skills, while formidable, aren't enough to go against four guards with pulse rifles. Plus, we have the young. We cannot both defend and attack with a single effective operator at once. There will also be reinforcements nearby. We must move fast enough to take the ship before others arrive, and I am unable to traverse the distance rapidly." His summary was clipped, professional, spoken with the confidence of years of battle.

"We could create a distraction?" offered Shari.

Lenora smiled at the young female. "While I appreciate the offer, it wouldn't work. Look at their eyes, their stance. The quality of their weapons and armor. They are professionals. They won't run off after an errant child or bolt at unexpected sounds." Shari examined the males with fresh eyes, seeing what Lenora pointed out. "We need subterfuge."

Lenora considered. "They are here for me. I will approach them and offer to talk to Trent. It's the only card we have to play. They won't kill me, not if he wants to talk."

Vordan gripped her arm. "That's insane. There's a lot of damage they can do before they get to killing you. You don't know what he'll do. You don't even know if he wants to talk! Maybe he's issued a kill on sight order. There has to be a better option."

"They haven't," piped Shari. "They want her alive."

"That's reassuring," responded Lenora dryly, and Shari looked at her as if she was nuts.

Vordan looked around, desperate to find another option. He cursed when all he saw were empty landing pads and unused cargo pallets. He banged his head back against the troop transport in frustration and paused. He looked up at the expanse of the vehicle.

"How long has this been here? Does it run?"

Lett shrugged. "It's owned by the Crows. They use it for weekly troop drills."

Vordan grinned. "So, it runs?"

Lett returned his grin, understanding. "It runs."

"Alright, Pirate Queen. New plan…"

***

Lenora stepped out from behind the troop transport, arms up. "Hello, boyos. Been a long time. Heard you're looking for me." The males instantly trained their guns on her. She continued her slow walk towards them. "Now now. No need for all that. You're looking for me, and I'm here."

"Where's the muscle?" one asked.

Lenora shrugged. "Got bit by a bug and died. Easy come, easy go. I'll get another when I go home."

One sniggered, and she pinned him with a stare. "Something funny there?"

"It's cute how you think you're going home," he replied, leering at her.

Her voice was crisp. "You really want to pick a fight with me? With the Oonaugh? Have you forgotten who I am? What we do to those that cross us? Surely, even in this shit-hole backwater, you aren't that naïve."

They stiffened at her tone, and she had to admit that she felt a frisson of pride. Even a decade later, they still knew her, feared her. "I am Lenorielle Oonaugh. I've killed more males than you've met in your life. Don't fuck with me."

"Heard you were on the outs with the family." This one was older, more seasoned. He examined her carefully, not buying her act. That wasn't good. She considered her options, decided to bluster her way through it.

She stiffened, made her voice harsher still. "The clan isn't in the habit of sharing our intel with country moonshiners."

"Lots of things changed in a decade. If you were back in, you'd know that. Crows have expanded. Got a lot more going on now." He cocked his head, his eyes hardening as he reached his decision. "You know, I think we might just take our chances. Trent wants a little chat, then I think we'll see if your daddy really will come to the rescue."

She hissed, drawing her gun lightning fast. "Careful, sweetheart. Remember what happened to the last lot that tried to abduct and hold an Oonaugh. I wiped them off the face of existence myself."

Behind her, she heard a low whine and smiled triumphantly. She whipped her gun around, firing wide with a low energy burst that wouldn't damage the shuttle, but created a lot of light and noise, then ducked. As she hit the ground, the gun turret on the troop transport activated and, in four precision strikes, took out the guards.

She hopped up and raced for the shuttle, hearing the shouts from the reinforcements as they barreled towards the landing bay to investigate the shots. The troop transport lumbered into the air in hover mode, less than a meter from the ground, and swung towards the shuttle.

She reached it first and ordered her HUD to open the airlock and start the engines. The troop transport pulled alongside the shuttle, providing cover for the kids and Vordan as they clambered out and into the shuttle.

She jumped into the pilot seat, Vordan slumping heavily into the co-pilot chair while the kids crammed into the small cargo area. Bizarrely, Shari seemed to be having the time of her life, grinning widely and whooping. Strange child.

"Can you fly this?" Vordan asked.

"Well enough for this," she replied grimly. "Just don't ask me to navigate anywhere off-planet."

The guards reached them as they were taking off and began shooting at the shuttle. Vordan closed his eyes, and the troop transport turret gun turned on the guards, laying down a blistering cover fire.

She laughed, delighted. "Is that you?"

He nodded, grinning, with his eyes still closed. "I connected my HUD to it before I left. Baby has remote control."

They took off smoothly into the air with no further interference. They flew in silence for several tense minutes, expecting pursuit, before they began to slowly relax. Vordan looked at Lenora, then the kids. "All alright?"

The kids nodded in unison before Shari piped up, "That was the awesomest thing ever. Totally bad ass." Lett nodded in support. Vordan grinned. It was the most age-appropriate thing he'd heard them say yet.

He turned to Lenora. "We made it. I can't believe that crazy plan worked."

She looked back at him for a long moment before she laughed. It was the kind of exhausted, half-crazy, half-relieved laugh that one makes after a traumatic event they aren't quite sure how to process. "That was seriously the most fun I've had in ages. Did you see their faces?" She cackled. "They were terrified! My legend precedes me!" The kids giggled along with her as she wiped the tears away. "Still got it!"

Vordan reached out to her, gripping her hand. "Yeah, you still got it." His eyes were warm, his appreciation honest and bright.

"What now, Pirate Queen?"

"Now, we drop the kids off with Ari and rendezvous with Casti." The kids went silent. It was like a stone dropped into a pond. "What? What's wrong? Wasn't that the deal? I can take you to the south space port in Rilaz. The Oonaugh will take you in. I wasn't kidding about my family. Ari, my sister, runs that outpost. They are always looking for smart young recruits."

The kids looked at each other, in another of those silent communications that she was beginning to think might be indicative of some sort of telepathy. It wasn't an uncommon skill, and trauma often accelerated the development of such things. "We want to go with you."

Lenora was stunned and took a moment to compose her thoughts. "Why?"

"Because you're... you. You're Elle Oonaugh. Even the Crows fear you. What you did there... that was totally bad ass. I wanna be like you. Please, teach me." Shari's voice was small, tentative. Unlike her usual mercenary manner.

"We are on a mission, Shari. It's not a safe place for children."

"Neither was the gamma sector. The Oonaugh won't be either."

Ok, she had a point there. "Those aren't your only options... we could find a school or something."

Lett looked at her like she had sprouted a second head. "What would we do in a school?"

Ok, again. Another point. "Look, I just don't think..."

"It's too late," Vordan cut in. "Casti is here."

Belatedly, Lenora realized that there was a ship approaching on the scanner. Zera's voice filled her HUD. "Hey, Sister. We decided to come get you in case Vordan needed medical assistance. We have the best MedBay in the universe onboard."

The bulk of Casti eclipsed the nearby stars, its gleaming black surface absorbing the light all around them as it swallowed them into the shuttle bay.

"Your sister owns that ship? Is this the same sister that runs the Oonaugh at the south port?" asked Lett, his voice hushed in awe.

"No, Zera isn't a blood sister. She is Falosian military, as am I. We are sisters by choice."

"You're Falosian military? I thought you were Oonaugh," asked Shari suspiciously.

Lenora shrugged. "I'm both." She caught herself by surprise; for the first time in her life, she thought that statement might actually be true.

Chapter Ten

The Pirate Queen

The moment they were given the all clear on Casti, they opened the hatch and disembarked. Lenora couldn't help but notice that the shuttle bay had been redesigned. Rather than the featureless matte black expanse that was Casti's default, it had been reformatted to look just like any other spaceship shuttle bay, lots of gray metal and studded deck plates.

Odran met them in the shuttle bay with a gurney, which Vordan was piled onto and whisked away. That left Zera, Lenora, and the kids.

"Who do we have here?" asked Zera.

Lenora made the introductions. "Perhaps we can go to the mess hall and feed the kids before we continue?" Truth be told, they looked like they were going to fall over. The reality of what they had just done was dawning on them, and she could sense their emotions careening from anxiety to hope, underlaid by a persistent exhaustion borne of living moment to moment for a long time.

Sub-vocally, Lenora spoke to Zera. "Did you redesign the ship?"

"Yes. If we are going to have strangers onboard, we can't give away that it's alien tech. I had a long discussion with Casti and uploaded specs for a state-of-the-art ship. It will mimic it for as long as we need.

No one will ever know that we are anything other than rich mercs with access to cutting edge tech."

Lenora nodded, grateful for Zera's foresight. She hadn't considered the danger she might have placed the kids in by bringing them here, exposing them to the secret of Casti. She mentally chastised herself. She had to be smarter than that.

They got the kids seated in the mess hall, their eyes wide at the truly astonishing amount of food Casti pulled out for them, and then settled themselves at a booth a little way away, so that they could converse in private.

"Will Vordan be ok?" asked Zera.

Lenora told her about the healer on the planet. "He just needs rest. We have a week before we need to show up at that auction. Plenty of time for a Verit to recover. For now, we need to head back to the South Port, drop off those kids, and borrow some of my sister's troops. I won't risk bringing in more Verit until we have to–I don't want to make it obvious who we are. A troop of mixed species will work better."

They finessed the details and sat exchanging small talk for a bit. Lucius and Denara hadn't checked in yet, so Zera and Odran had little info to provide.

"You've done well, Lenora. I know this must have been difficult for you."

Lenora sighed, sitting back in the booth. "It was. Harder than I thought. But also... nice. I got to see my Melati. And... honestly, it was fun being Elle Oonaugh. She never gave a shit what anyone thought. I think I forgot, somehow, that there were good bits as well as bad to being her."

Eventually, the kids grew tired. Lenora was filled with a relentless drive to seek out Vordan, to check he was ok. She told herself that it was because he was assigned to her, her responsibility, but she knew she was lying to herself. She missed him. Worried about him. Somehow, amongst all his banter, she had grown feelings for him. She wasn't quite sure how or when he had sneaked in under her guard, but it had happened and there was no point in denying it. She knew she wouldn't rest until she checked on him.

She walked the kids to their assigned quarters, assuring them she could be contacted at any time through the ship's comms. Then she went to MedBay. *Just for a peek,* she told herself.

She crept quietly into the room. Casti had dimmed the lights to allow Vordan to sleep, and there was a soft, warm yellow glow around the base of the wall, providing just enough light not to trip on anything. He lay on a large bed, designed for Verit proportions. A display above the bed showed his vitals, but she wasn't medical enough to know what they meant. He looked peaceful, sleeping. When he was awake, he flitted from charm to humor to intensity, but sleeping, he looked young and carefree. She turned to go, leaving him to his rest, when he spoke quietly into the dimness.

"I know you're there. I can hear you."

"Sorry. I wasn't trying to wake you. I just wanted to check you were alright."

"It's fine. You can come in." He sighed, and there was a rustling sound. "I've made sure everything is decently covered."

Shame, her mind whispered, and she admonished herself with a mental kick. *He's just survived poisoning, and you're creeping on him.* Could she get any tackier?

"How do you feel?" She moved to sit on the side of the bed. She had to hop a little to get onto it, it was so high.

"Better. Not so much like I might meet the Goddess at any second."

"That's good then." They sat quietly in the dark, in a peaceful cocoon of dim light. "I was worried we'd lost you there for a minute." She was aiming for light, but her voice caught. She couldn't quite hide the bone chilling fear that had filled her.

"Hey, hey. It's ok." His big warm hand reached out and captured hers. "I'm here, I'm fine."

"You nearly weren't!" she hissed. "You nearly died." She was appalled to hear herself sniff, to feel wetness on her cheeks. Oh, blessed Goddess, she was crying.

"I know." His words were solemn. "I'm sorry. For my carelessness. I didn't mean to worry you. It won't happen again." His palm ran up her shoulder to cup her cheek as he spoke.

"Don't apologize to me! Be careful for yourself." She tried to pull away, but instead he pulled her down to lie next to him.

"Can we not fight just now, just this once?" he asked. "I'm injured, you know."

She laughed, a wet sound. "It's your own fault. I should kick your ass for not following orders."

"But then you might damage my ass. It'd be a crime to your sisters everywhere."

She tsked him but didn't deny it. She had spent entirely too long admiring him, and she wouldn't lie. To him or herself. She allowed herself to lie there, tucked up against him, and relax. She took her first deep breath since he had been injured and let herself soak in his warmth. She let herself believe he was alive, that he'd make it. She placed her hand on his chest, pressing against the crisp hairs edging out of the top of his medical gown, and let herself feel his heartbeat thrumming under her fingertips.

He rubbed soothing circles on her back until she felt like she was boneless, the tension melting away. She couldn't pinpoint exactly when she felt the energy shift. Felt the mood darken slightly into something richer. She caught the tendrils of lust in his emotional resonance. Felt his awareness of her closeness ignite. His hand moved down to the small of her back, pressing her against him, his other hand crossing over to the nape of her neck, pulling her to him.

"Lenora...?" His voice was rough. "Say no, lady, if this is not what you want."

They paused, balanced on the knife edge of decision. He waited, his desire plain, letting the choice be hers. It was an aphrodisiac, like nothing else could have been. She surged forward, sealing their mouths together. His tongue delved into hers, tasting, surging in and out.

He pulled her half over him, his big palms roaming her body. He groaned into the kiss, and she froze. "Are you alright? Did I hurt you?"

"No." He tugged at her outfit impatiently. "I am well. How in the name of the Goddess do I get this thing off you?"

She laughed and kneeled back on the bed, shucking off her coat and jacket, before shimmying out of her jumpsuit pants. He groaned again when he saw her, silhouetted, naked against the dim light. He froze for a second.

"Casti?"

"Yes?"

"Lock the door."

"Yes, Vordan."

She laughed, a deep rich sound, and came back down onto him. He palmed her breasts, surprised at their fullness, her nipples peaking into his hands. He suckled one, then the other in turn, tugging with his teeth as he scraped delicately. It was Lenora's turn to moan as she let him lead the dance.

"What is that?" she whispered, panting.

"What?" he murmured as he admired the pretty raspberry color of her nipples.

"The roughness."

He chuckled darkly. "Cat, remember?" She didn't reply as he laved her again. He unsheathed his claws just a little and trailed them gently over her ass, feeling the soft dimples and curves.

"My turn." She shimmied back, pulling his covers down with her. He half sat up, clawing off the medical gown before reclining back onto the cushions, naked. He shouted in surprise when she pulled him free and pulled him into her mouth, taking him deep, without warning.

"Have mercy, lady." He panted.

"No," she replied, grinning wickedly, as she licked him again from base to tip before blowing gently on the wetness and swallowing him again. She tortured him, teasing him with tongue and teeth until he couldn't take any more. Grabbing her hair, he pulled her off him with a pop and up to his mouth to claim another wet, hot kiss. He reached down for her, feeling her wetness, stroking his fingers over the excruciatingly sensitive apex of her thighs. She groaned as he pushed his fingers inside before pushing his hand away, impatient. There would be time for gentle later.

Lenora positioned herself over him, and impaled herself in a single rush, moaning as she felt the burning stretch as he filled her. When he was fully seated, she paused. She leaned forward, bracing herself on his chest, and pressed another kiss to his lips. "Just give me a minute," she whispered against his lips.

"As long as you need," he promised. He reached down, massaging her ass and lower back, helping her relax into him, luxuriating in the sensations of her pressed along the length of him. When she was ready, she moved. She rode him, getting used to his size, as they learned each other's rhythm. It was sweet, he realized. Sweet and generous, so like the female in his arms. So unexpected. She took and gave in equal measure. He let her set the pace initially until he couldn't hold back. He gripped her hips, pulling her hard into him, pounding into her with a desire to make them one. It was furious and raw as they met each other thrust for thrust.

She screamed her release into the cocooning darkness around them, and as she did, she connected them. She shared the exquisite joy, the flood of sensations, the colorful explosion in her mind. It pushed him over the edge as well and he roared into her, holding her tight as they shuddered together. It was the most incredible thing he had ever experienced. In all his years, nothing could have prepared him for the searing intimacy of their heart-mind bond, of feeling the exquisite pain-pleasure of their joining.

They lay there afterwards, sweat cooling on their bodies. He pulled the covers over them, and she snuggled close, sharing their body heat. Deep in his mind, he could still feel her, like a warm blaze.

"That was... incredible."

"Mhhm," she murmured sleepily.

"I didn't know Falosians could do that."

"Only sometimes," she mumbled. "Both people need to fit right. Special." Her breath evened out as she fell into sleep. He lay there, watching her. Unable to believe how much the firmament of his universe had shifted so unexpectedly in such a short space of time. She was right, it was special. So was she.

Nothing to date had prepared him for Lenorielle. She was a mass of contradictions, and he adored her in all of her guises.

When Lenora woke up the next morning, she was lying on her side in a Falosian style room, all pale wood paneling and dark jewel toned furnishings. She couldn't remember how she had got there. The last thing she remembered was falling asleep on the big medical bed with Vordan. She was deliciously warm, and it took a moment to realize it was because Vordan was curled around her. His thigh was pressed between hers, his palm on her breast.

Well, this is unexpected.

"So, do we pretend it didn't happen?" murmured Vordan as he nestled deeper into her hair.

Everything in her screamed in instant rejection. "No. Not unless you want to."

He curved his arm around her, pulling her closer to him. "No. I don't want to." He pulled the covers up higher, tucking her in. "But I do need another few hours of sleep. I nearly died yesterday, remember? Then a certain pirate queen jumped my bones."

She huffed out a laugh. "I don't remember doing any jumping. I think I was the jumpee, not the jumper."

"You took advantage of my accommodating nature."

She laughed aloud. "Poor baby. Your injured virtue." She snuggled down under the covers. "Thank you for last night. It was incredible."

He pressed a kiss to her temple. "It was," he agreed. "But you don't need to thank me. It wasn't a favor." He paused. "I can still feel you, you know. In my mind, just a little."

"It'll fade away," she responded, quietly. "With time." She paused again. "That kind of bond takes either constant reinforcement and repetition, or a deep soul connection."

She could feel Vordan weighing up her answer. "What happens if there is repetition?"

Her breath caught, and she rolled over to look at his face. Her gaze traveled over his features, so familiar to her now. His high cheekbones, the slash of his dark brows. "Do you want it to happen again?"

He caught her gaze, the tension between them electric. "Yes. I don't know what this is between us yet, but I want it to happen again. I want to know you, Lenora. Inside and out. I want to know Elle, Lenora, Lenorielle, the Black Valkyrie. All of your faces. These past days have been the most intense, incredible experience of my life. I have felt more alive with you than I've felt in years. So yes, if you'll allow it, I want to do this again and again until we know what we are to each other."

Lenora was stunned. She couldn't speak. She had felt his growing admiration, sensed his flashes of lust. But even their stolen kiss in the Red Wing hadn't prepared her for this. The emotions she sensed, his words, spoke of something much, much deeper. She gave herself time to consider. Really consider how she felt. He had spoken with such soul bearing honesty, she would not disrespect him with anything less.

Did she want to do this again? She was highly attracted to him, physically and mentally. She had caught herself staring at him, thinking about him, more times than she could count. But was it more than that? Somewhere along the way, their fake relationship had transformed into something more real. She relied on him, trusted him implicitly. When she had thought he might die...

"Yes. I want to do this again. I don't know what this is, but the thought of losing you to the bug venom... my life without you in it would be infinitely sadder." She trailed a fingertip along his jaw. "I am not afraid to explore this. I cannot give you any promises, but I'm open to exploring where we go from here."

His eyes heated. "I look forward to the challenge of finding you, Elle."

She smiled at him in invitation. "Are you still tired?"

He pulled her under him with a squeak and a laugh. "Not anymore, lady."

The galaxy could wait another couple of hours.

Chapter Eleven

Can I Borrow a Cup of Sugar?

Lenora called Ari, explaining the situation.

"You want me to do what?" Ari's voice was incredulous.

"Look after a couple of kids and loan me some personnel for a few days."

"That's what I thought you said. Do I look like a babysitter?"

"Don't be like that. The kids are smart. You know Oonaugh always has a place for smart kids."

Ari hissed out a breath. "Urgh. Fine. Bring them by the temple. How many people do you want?"

"Just a few. I need to put on a show, and I need some muscle."

Ari was instantly suspicious. "Is this for the auction?"

"Yes. At the casino in Valhalla. I'll return them in a week or so."

Ari considered. "Alright. I'll give you a few. But I want you to take Luta."

It was Lenora's turn to be taken aback. "Really? Why? Luta is a sect leader; they have their own operations. Surely they've got better things to do than play at muscle."

"I'm worried about you. You've been out of the game for a while, Sister. I'd feel better if you had them with you."

Lenora sighed. "Fine. I'll be there soon."

The trip to Haven had been blessedly uneventful. The kids had gone into Ari's care sullenly, exchanged for three muscle-bound clan members and Luta. The Oonaugh clan members had mostly kept to themselves, staying in their rooms, emerging only for food and to use the gym.

Vordan and her had taken the opportunity to get to know each other better, and it was... nice. Ok scratch that. It was outstanding. He was sweet, funny and a generous lover. They learned each other and danced around the fact that they were both much more involved than they cared to admit.

On the second day, Lenora woke without Vordan by her side. It was the first time she had woken alone since that first night in the MedBay. She was disorientated for a second, so used to waking with his warm presence wrapped around her. It scared her, how quickly she had become used to him, to his stupid jokes and joy for life. He laughed constantly, such a contrast to her own intense nature.

Frustrated with herself, she pulled on her workout gear and bundled her hair up in a bun and headed for the gym. With others onboard, Casti was limited to providing only what was available on any state-of-the-art cruiser. She picked a recording of a series of Delma-Ley-At stretches and projected it onto the wall display. Pulling out a couple of mats, she joined in, copying the precise moves while her mind drifted. Time and time again, she found herself thinking of him. It began to infuriate her, how much space he occupied in her mind. She was on a high-priority mission for her people, and she was mooning over a male. It was almost comical. Neither Elle nor Lenora would have approved of her preoccupation.

Elle would have teased her, and told her to bang his brains out until he was out of her system. Lenora would have scolded her and told her to focus on her job. Right now, she wasn't sure who she was, and that scared her even more.

These past few weeks had taken her life on a sharp right turn, and she felt like the sand was moving beneath her feet. Who was she? The military officer? A daughter of Oonaugh? In the middle of her musing, she missed a step in the stretching, miscalculated her move and landed face first on the mat, unbalanced. Well, if that wasn't a metaphor for her life, she didn't know what was.

She heard the door open behind her, and didn't need to turn to see who it was. Her whole body was attuned to him, his emotional resonance familiar in her mind. Vordan stepped in and stopped when he saw her lying face-first.

"Are you alright?"

She didn't move. "Yes. Just contemplating my life."

"Ah ha." He hovered in the doorway. "Would you like some privacy for that, or a help up?"

She flopped over to lie on her back, staring at the ceiling. "You can come in. I don't want to interrupt your workout. It's plenty big for both of us."

He came over and crouched next to her. "Can I help with anything?"

Lenora shook her head, appalled to realize that she was blinking back tears. "Nope. Just being moody."

He lay next to her on the mat. "I don't mind."

"Really, Vordan. I'm all snarled up in my head today. I'm not good company."

He rolled onto his side, looking at her, his head propped up on his elbow. "I'll leave you be, if that's what you really want." He paused, examining her face, and she closed her eyes, afraid that he'd see too much in them. "But when I feel like that, a good sparring session helps. Want to try?"

Her eyes shot open. "Really?" She couldn't hide the excitement in her voice.

"Really. I have had little chance to spar in Delma-Ley-At yet. I promise to keep my claws sheathed." He pressed his hand over his heart solemnly but couldn't hide the twinkling of his eyes. Dammit, he had her, and he knew it.

Lenora stretched again and sat up. "Deal. I've tried calming stretches, and they didn't work. Let's try working it out a bit more vigorously."

He winked at her. "I mean, if that's what you want..."

"I mean sparring, Flyboy. Don't get over-excited." She grinned at him and jumped up, grabbing another couple of mats to expand their fight area. Vordan did a couple of stretches to limber up and assumed the sparring stance.

"Come on, Pirate Queen. Let's see what you've got," he taunted.

She stilled for a moment, gathering her energy, before she took off. She swiped a low kick, blindingly fast, that swept his knees out from under him, delivering a barrage of blows to his shoulders, face, and upper torso as he went down. She pulled her punches, barely more than taps, and laughed in delight when she saw his shocked expression.

"First round to me!" she sang out, bouncing on the balls of her feet.

He got to his feet again, ready for the next round. "My lady, you are full of surprises." he practically purred at her. Vordan crossed sideways around the edge of the mat, and she felt his energy shift as he stalked her.

"If by surprise, you mean where I outright told you I am skilled in hand-to-hand combat, then sure," she teased, watching his eyes rather than his footsteps. She saw his eyes flick to the left, and she dove right, ready to avoid his attack, and walked right into it. She cursed as he grabbed her hip and shoulder and threw her. She landed on the floor on her back with a heavy "Ooof!" and he came down over her, twisting her arm and leg into submission position.

He patted her hair with his free hand, avoiding a snapping bite from her. "Don't be a sore loser, lady. You fell for my feint." He tapped her on the nose in reprimand. "Second round to me. One all."

He let her go, and they both stood up again, this time more cautious, more aware of the other's strengths. Vordan began to stalk again, and Lenora considered her options. Stalking was predatory behavior. If she let him, he would own the game. The best defense is a good offence. The next time he took a step, rather than moving away from him, she attacked. She swept at his lagging foot while he was in motion, forcing him to dance back.

It was on. They traded blows back and forth as they waltzed across the mat, evenly matched, never quite able to get the other one. It was glorious. As they moved, she felt her muscles loosen, her tension drain away with the sweat trickling down her back. She was pleased to see that he was having to work to keep up with her, his brow shining as he worked out. Her focus narrowed to just her and Vordan, the mats and their private contest. Nothing else existed except Lenora and Vordan, in perfect sync.

It ended suddenly. Lenora went to counter a move but misjudged her timing and had to twist sharply to avoid hitting him outright, wrenching her shoulder in the process. She disengaged and cursed, massaging her injured shoulder.

Vordan came up to her, examining her injury, his jaw tight. "That looks painful." He went to the gym MedBag and returned with a small tissue repair device, having her sit in front of him on the mat while he applied it to her shoulder.

"That feels amazing, thank you." Lenora hung her head forward, letting the soothing energy from the repair device flow through her shoulder.

"You'll need to be more careful next time if we spar again. I don't like hurting females."

She shrugged with her other shoulder. "It was an accident, that's all. Don't make a big deal out of it. Besides, I had you in that last round."

He laughed slightly. "Only because you were cheating, lady."

Lenora was stunned and turned to look at him over her shoulder in confusion. "What? How? We're sparring. How can I possibly be cheating?"

He nudged her head back forward so that he could continue to treat her injury. "You were predicting my moves. You used your empathy."

Her denial was immediate, her disappointment in him bitter in her mouth. She wouldn't have thought that Vordan would react badly to being bested. "No, I wasn't. I was just anticipating you."

He stared at her. "That last round, on three different occasions you were moving to counter before I had consciously decided to move."

"Maybe I'm just that good," she retorted, hurt that he would accuse her.

"Then why can I feel our bond active in my mind? It feels like when we are mating."

Lenora let out her breath in a rush and felt for their bond. He was right; it was active. Vibrant and open, in a way that she had never encountered before. She was instantly contrite. "I'm sorry, Vordan. I didn't realize."

Why hadn't she realized? Then it hit her. She was so used to him. They had spent too much time together, the bond had slowly become more solid. Over the past few days, it had grown in tiny increments so that it was nearly always present. Her energy and focus during the sparring had forced it open from a thread of connection to a wide conduit. It was what happened... to mated couples. Some developed a type of telepathy, others just a general awareness of where the other was and how they were feeling.

"It's alright. I don't mind, it's nice feeling you there. Although it gives you an unfair advantage when we spar." He felt her tension. "What's wrong? Is it a problem?"

She swallowed her shock. "It's unusual. It doesn't normally develop this fast. Couples spend years developing this kind of bond. I'm sorry, it crept up on me and I didn't notice it."

Vordan crawled around from behind to face her. "It is a problem?" he repeated. "Why do you sound so scared? I told you I don't mind."

She had to tell him, had to be honest. "It is the start of a mating bond." His eyes widened in shock. "It usually requires a deliberate choice on both sides. I've never heard of it growing like this, and in just a few days."

"I see." He considered. "What does it mean? Is it harmful?"

She shook her head. "It's just... awareness. Connection. It brings couples closer together."

He reached out and took her hand. "Is it permanent?"

She shook her head again. "Like any psychic connection, it takes energy and proximity to maintain. It would fade over time if we chose not to continue."

He cocked his head at her. "What's the problem? If it's not harmful, and it's not permanent, then what's the issue?"

She tried to pull her hand away, but he resisted her. "On Falosia, it is considered a significant breach of ethics to form a psychic connection with someone without their consent." She was embarrassed and appalled at herself. "It is a violation."

"But I thought you said both parties had to consent for this type of bond to happen?" She nodded reluctantly. "So how do you know I didn't? Perhaps sub-consciously I did." She had no answer for that.

He drew her closer to him, pulled her into his lap. "Don't worry about it. If you had asked me, I would have consented."

She snarled at him. "That's not how consent works."

"Why are you picking a fight about this? I just told you it's not a problem. What are you terrified of?"

It terrified her all over again, how well he truly saw and understood her. "It is a mating bond."

"I know. You said. Why does that scare you?"

"I never thought I would be mated. I went to the colony for Maral, never expecting to find someone. I've never allowed myself to be in this position before."

Vordan chose his words carefully. "Is it the concept of mating that scares you? Or being mated to me?"

Lenora's breath caught in her throat. Of all the ways that she had thought her morning would go, discussing mating was not one of them. "Honestly? I don't know. This is moving very fast. We haven't even known each other two weeks. Is this even what you want?"

Vordan touched her cheek and pulled her close to him, kissing her lightly on the lips. "In the interests of the same honesty, lady, I don't know either." He pressed butterfly kisses along her cheek, up her temple, and nuzzled her hair. "I've never been in this position before."

He wrapped his arms around her waist and pulled her to sit more fully over him, her legs around his hips.

"I know that I adore you, Lenora." Her breath caught. "You are the most incredible female I have ever met. You are fire and ice and a whirlwind that has turned my life upside down. The last two weeks have been the best of my life."

"You almost died three days ago from poison!" she accused.

He grinned at her. "It was worth it. It brought me to my first night with you."

She laughed. "I think you are a bit mad, Vordan."

He pulled her closer, nibbling his way down her neck. "Let's just see where it goes. Nothing has changed. I adore you. I don't want this to end, and I love your freaky psychic bond."

She twisted his braids in her hands and pulled him up to claim a lush, wet kiss. "I adore you as well, Flyboy. I don't know how, but in the last few days, you've suddenly become essential to my life."

There was a gentle ping, and Casti spoke into their HUDs. "Excuse my interruption, but I thought you might want to know that several of the Oonaugh clan are on their way to the gym. ETA thirty seconds."

They laughed together, and he stroked his way down to her hips and ass for a last squeeze. "We are always finding ourselves in compromising positions in public spaces."

"Later," she promised, pressing a final kiss to him before she disentangled.

"Later," he agreed.

When the Oonaugh males arrived just a few seconds later, they were ready for another sparring session.

Chapter Twelve

The Red Sea

The past few days had been a gentle respite in their mission, but it was over now. Lenora stood at the gaudy entrance of the Red Sea Casino, ready for the next step in their assignment. The Red Sea Casino was as horrific as she had expected. On Valhalla colony, anything went. The casino pulsed with alien music and seared her eyeballs with garish flashing lights. It felt about a million degrees, and the smell of thousands of beings assaulted her nose until she wanted to gag. She couldn't imagine how much worse it would be to Vordan.

Nothing of her discomfort showed on the outside. She glided through the throng, her guards forming a wedge around her. Between her sister's loaners and Odran, Zera, and Vordan, she had her own personal pack of killers. They did a good job of glaring menacingly at anyone that took a split second too long to get out of the way.

She had to admit, they looked dangerous. Everyone had dressed dramatically in black, head to toe. Her sixteen-year-old self would have loved it, and the Vicious Crows might have expired on the spot from sheer jealousy.

As for Vordan, her temperature had shot into the stratosphere when she saw him. He looked flat out, hands down hot. When he had emerged from the bathroom in their chambers in his outfit, she had promptly divested him of it and made them an hour late to a briefing. He was completely recovered from his illness. His iron-gray hair shined against the black, and his pale skin made him look particularly menacing. He prowled alongside her, on her right, looking every inch the feline he was under the skin.

Lenora herself had also gone with the theme, head to toe in black leather. Her pants and vest were threaded with nano steel fibers, making them bullet, blade, and pulse weapon resistant. Her shirt was smooth black si-silk, designed to resist scanning by all known technologies. She put her hair up into a crown braid in case she had to fight. Underneath it all, she wore a black military Falosian bodysuit. It monitored her vitals, kept her warm or cool, and would keep her alive even if she had to jump out of an airlock. They were as prepared as they could be.

As she walked, she took several deep breaths, calming herself and stuffing all her anxiety down. For the next few hours, she must be Lenorielle Oonaugh. Pirate Queen in truth. She must project complete self-assurance. She loosened her tight muscles, allowed herself to glide along the floor, arrogant, confident, strong.

Vordan cast her a quick glance, sensing the change, and his lips quirked slightly in understanding. He shortened his step to match hers. They prowled together in perfect sync, the ultimate criminal gang power couple. Ready to tear through their enemies as a team. She sniggered internally. She had been going for dangerous-assassin-couple and somehow ended up in a cute Bonnie and Clyde style rom-com.

They probably looked like an ad for "Bad-Guys-Are-Us." Or some sort of expensive BDSM clothing shop.

Eventually, they arrived at the Ruby Room. The auction was due to begin within the hour. She held her breath when she gave her name to the looming guard at the door, but he simply scanned her credentials and waved her and her party inside. The Ruby Room was smaller than she had expected, just an average size conference hall with maybe a hundred or so others there before her. They were grouped into their respective factions, standing in little circles holding little drinks and... canapes? How civilized.

The room was surprisingly tasteful, given the rest of the casino, all dark smoked glass and dark wood. She walked in and went to the bar on the opposite wall, ordering a drink for herself. The others assumed a guard stance. Every move was tactical, considered. Their stance signaled their professionalism. They weren't some random merc group here to chow down on pastries; they were professional soldiers.

Lenora prowled the room, her guard and Vordan following her. She saw several people she knew from her past dealings. Each had a similar reaction, their eyes casting over her, assessing a new competitor, before shooting back to her face in recognition, their eyes widening in shock.

The first to speak to her was ancient Wilhelma, leader of a very successful deep space crew. They specialized in remote space logistics disruption. Ancient though she may be, she was shrewd. Her single glance noted the professional soldiers, high-tech weaponry, and Luta on loan from the main Oonaugh clan. That one look told her everything. Lenora was back, she was serious, and her family supported her. She bowed slightly, giving her a wide, welcoming smile. "If it isn't Elle Oonaugh. Where have you been, love? It's been terribly boring without you."

She smiled back. She'd always had a soft spot for the elder female, evil bitch that she was. "Wilhelma! I'm pleased to see that no one has killed you yet."

Wilhelma smiled toothily. "Luta. It's not often we see you out either these days. Have you finally decided to leave the Oonaugh?"

Luta turned her silver gaze on Wilhelma, holding the ancient's eyes long enough to make her feel uncomfortable before she spoke. "Elle is Oonaugh." She turned away, dismissing Wilhelma, and joined the others standing guard.

Wilhelma cackled. "Ah, still a creature of few words. It's amazing how much she manages to say, with so little."

Lenora nodded. It was. With just three words and her mere presence, Luta had told the world that Elle was back, and she was supported by the might of the Oonaugh clan. Lenora made a mental note to thank her sister later. "How's Drigu?"

Wilhelma's laugh boomed. "Well, retired now. The twins have taken over most of the work. Enjoying playing with the grandchildren."

"That sounds divine. What are you doing here, rather than sunning yourself on some beach with your wife?"

"Training my successor." She motioned to a hulking young male. "You remember Dvuant? He's taking over."

Lenora nodded and smiled politely. "Nice to see you again." The poor male looked entirely out of his depth, like he would rather be bashing heads than holding tiny drinks and even smaller pastries.

"Dvuant, Elle here is the best in the business at quick, efficient stealth jobs. Logistics, special acquisitions, assassinations... She's the real deal. Don't screw her over, and she'll deliver every time."

Lenora looked at Wilhelma in surprise. "That's a big recommendation coming from you."

She shrugged. "It is the truth. These new ones, they don't understand how the business works." She waved a gnarled hand at the room. "They think it's all 'shoot them up, make a splash.' Those of us that have been at this the longest, we know the value of professionalism."

"Thank you. As it happens, I am starting a new venture. This is Vordan." She ran her hand up his arm to rest on his shoulder. "He's ex-Tothas. We are putting together a new group, focusing on logistics, acquisitions, and tactical space warfare strikes. If you are in the market, please contact us." She held out her other hand, projecting her contact information above her palm.

Wilhelma nodded, pleased, and scanned her info. She scrutinized Vordan. "Is this your new mate, then? What happened to the crow boy?"

Vordan laughed and wrapped an arm around Lenora's waist. "They were just warming my seat."

The elder nodded approvingly, giving him a gimlet eye. "Perhaps you can keep up with her, at that."

They stood in silence, sipping their drinks. Occasionally, another representative would come up to greet her, but all remained calm until Trent walked in. She saw him the instant he came through the door. He looked around, spotted her, and made a beeline towards them.

"Incoming," Vordan whispered, under the guise of reaching over to grab another canape.

"Shit. This isn't gonna be good," she murmured to Vordan.

Vordan flicked a glance at him. "He's very dramatic. Look at the way his cloak billows as he walks."

"Almost as dramatic as us, dressed all in our black head to toe leather." Vordan chuckled under his breath, blanking his face as Trent approached.

He spoke without preamble. "Elle. Imagine my surprise when my people told me you were back and had come to the old neighborhood to visit. I was so disappointed when you declined my invitation."

Lenora cocked her head at him, examining him like a curious bug that had crawled onto her salad. "Are you delusional?" Her voice was even, conversational. "Have you hit your head? You didn't invite me to visit. You shot at me and my team and tried to kidnap me."

"Just a misunderstanding," he replied smoothly. "We have history. The boyos know how much I've been looking forward to seeing you again. They wanted to surprise me."

Vordan snort-laughed, and Trent fixed him with a laser glare.

Vordan bared his teeth, in what could, on a dark night, possibly have been interpreted as a grin. "Do you always need your boys to find a female for you? If you have to kidnap them, you should take the hint that your technique needs work, mate. If you ask nicely, I'll give you some pointers." Vordan widened his grin, lengthening his incisors as he did, giving Trent a wink.

Trent looked him up and down before settling his mouth into a flat line. "Verit," he spat. "That's about right. You live under the heel of your females." He turned to Lenora. "What's wrong? You can't cope with a real male, you had to find a puppy dog that comes when you call?"

He waited expectantly, obviously hoping that his barb would result in some reaction. Instead, Lenora simply leaned into Vordan, and remained silent. Together, they stared him down until the silence became awkward. Trent turned back to Vordan. "What, you won't even defend your female? Some male."

Vordan cocked an eye at him. "My lady is quite capable of defending herself. She will ask if she needs my assistance. Clearly, you don't know her at all if you think she needs my help with a pathetic little birdy like you."

Lenora leaned over and kissed Vordan on the cheek. She reached out with her senses gently and realized that he meant every word. He adored her, was furious at Trent and wanted nothing more than to rip him limb from limb, but he had complete faith in her ability to deal with it. It warmed her, soothed a fear that she hadn't been consciously aware of, brought down another barrier between them.

"Go away, Trent. Before you embarrass yourself more. There's nothing for you here."

His face deepened into a dark purple. "You bitch, you're just like those Verit Maman. Expect a male to come crawling to you-"

His words were cut short when Vordan casually reached over and gripped him by the throat, lifting him off his feet and up to eye level with him. "Now, little bird. My lady can defend herself, but the Verit Maman are not here, so honor demands that I must." He squeezed, enjoying the panic in the male's eyes. "What did you have to say about the Verit Maman?" He shook the crow contemptuously. "As if a Maman of Verit would ever deign to give her time to something like you. Pathetic, honorless males capable of giving nothing. Hollow shells of your forefathers who would be ashamed at how far you have fallen. You leach on the lives of your females, on their energy and attention and care, and bring nothing in return."

Lenora unwound her belt and flicked it, uttering the alien command Vordan had taught her. On the other side, Luta pulled a pair of matched particle guns and aimed them at the other Crows that were preparing to defend their leader.

Vordan casually tossed Trent onto the floor where he flopped, gasping. "I will give you a gift, little bird. Something to help you remember the Maman of Verit, and my Queen here. For the next time you consider disrespecting a female."

Vordan extended the claws on his right hand and, with two quick swipes, shredded the male's shirt and jacket, exposing his lean chest. He took a single claw and began carving into his chest. The little bird screamed and tried to wriggle away, reaching for his guns at his hips, but Vordan simply placed a foot on each wrist and sat on his victim to keep him pinned. As he carved, he spoke calmly. "This gift is the symbol of the Goddess, of the divine feminine. Remember this, next time you decide to cause harm to a female."

When he was finished, he stood up, flicking the blood off of his talons contemptuously at the male's face, wiping his hands on the ragged shirt. Lenora watched him surface from the place of cold rage he had wandered to and register her and Luta holding the other Crows back.

He motioned to the nearest Crow. "Take him. If you come near us again, we'll kill you. Consider this a friendly warning."

The crows cautiously approached their leader, still moaning on the ground, and hauled him to his feet. Vordan watched as they left, before turning to the assembled crowd. "Is there anyone else that would like to discuss a matter with Madam Oonaugh?"

Hastily, they all resumed their own conversations. However, she saw several nods towards them. Apparently, to gain the respect of criminal gangs, all you had to do was torture someone on the floor of their fancy casino conference room. She caught Luta's gaze and was astonished to see Luta wink at her. Apparently Vordan had a fan in her as well.

Lenora reached out to a passing waiter and grabbed a drink and a napkin. She lifted Vordan's hand and gently dabbed the remaining flecks of blood away. "Are you alright?" she asked.

"Perfectly," he responded.

"That was a lot. Is there something I need to know?"

He stopped her dabbing and caught her gaze. "No. I'm fine." He paused, letting the dark stranger fill his eyes. "You should know, if we are going to continue this, that this is part of me. I will never accept disrespect, of you or the Maman. I am not capable of standing by and letting it pass. If you can't deal with that, say now. Before we go any deeper."

She held his gaze without flinching. "I told you, within a day of meeting you, that I deliberately blew up an entire base of people because they harmed my sister. Do you really think that I am squeamish? That a little blood will scare me off?" She smiled and downed her drink, feeling the burn as it crawled in her throat.

He didn't smile back. "Lady. I don't think much of anything scares you." He kissed her. It was deceptively gentle, full of promise, and it sent her up in flames. Vordan the flyboy was funny and sweet, but this male, Vordan the fighter... He was hot, dangerous and protective, and he spoke to the Elle in her, as much as the flyboy did.

She broke their kiss, twining her hands in his hair to hold him in place. "Certainly not you, Vordan. I see you, all of you, feel your emotions. Nothing about you scares me. Not your anger, your violence, nothing. I want all of you." She meant it, every word, and it felt right. Down to the bottom of her soul.

He locked eyes with her, nodding once, slowly.

A low gong echoed through the room, and the attendees turned towards the back wall, which lightened to a bright white. An automated voice spoke, "Attendees. Two minutes. Bidders log on."

A holo-projection appeared, and Lenora quickly scanned it with her HUD, logging in as the organization they had set up. On the screen, the registered participants appeared on a list on the right side. There were a dozen or so in the room, and approximately the same number remote bidding. Their listed name appeared–Valkyrie Arms.

On the left, a list of jobs appeared. Lenora felt a frisson of excitement. She had expected to have to wait weeks for this, take smaller jobs to build up her credibility. But here, at the first auction, there it was. The name of the group that had landed troops on Falosia, MUSHIT. They had posted a job.

The process was simple: each job was called in turn, the participants bidding at auction, with the selected bidder receiving a confirmation packet and further instructions.

Lenora bid on a few jobs, some more aggressively than others, to avoid suspicion, taking care not to win each.

Eventually, their target job came up. There were few details; a deep space seizure, loot and destroy mission. The bidding was heated, but they won, undercutting the nearest bid by only a small amount. It wasn't that unusual. Most people would expect a new company to low-ball to get some jobs under their belt. She resisted the urge to cheer when she received the confirmation packet. She couldn't quite believe it; it seemed too easy. After everything that had happened, it was anti-climactic.

They decamped immediately to Casti, marching through the casino as if it was enemy territory. They couldn't risk another interaction with the Crows when they finally had a lead.

Chapter Thirteen

Pirate Theater in the Sky

They reached Casti with no further encounters. After settling the Oonaugh guards in the mess hall with plenty of drinks, the colony team met on the bridge, where Lenora loaded up the packet to display it on the screens. Lenora waited, her stomach knotted with tension as Casti decrypted the data. Vordan slipped his hand into hers, giving it a gentle squeeze of support.

"We've got this. It'll be alright."

"There's no going back from this, Vordan. We have to do whatever this says to go any further. They could tell us to kidnap, murder, steal... anything." She sighed. "Even if we are doing it for the greater good, for our planets and home, that won't mean shit to the people that we harm in the process. They'll be just as dead."

The files opened, and a series of star maps scrawled across the displays, along with a date, time, and ship number. It looked familiar... Vordan began to laugh. "It's the next logistics ship, bound for the colony. They want us to make it disappear without a trace."

Lenora gaped. "That's... that's brilliant. We were already planning for a decoy ship that we can blow up." She whooped and Vordan picked her up by her waist, spinning her in a circle. "No one needs to get hurt!"

Vordan grinned. "And it's more proof that whoever the buyer is, it's the person we've been looking for. It's another thread tying them to the colony sabotage."

"There is one drawback, though," countered Zera. "My mission is a bust. Odran and I were supposed to chase back whoever was attacking the next logistics ship. If it's you, that mission is dead. That means that all our eggs are in one basket now with this."

Lenora was undaunted. "We'll make it work. We have no other choice."

***

Zera contacted the Dagger Kiss to make the arrangements for the decoy and dropped their muscle and Luta back at Rilaz with their thanks. When the time came, Lenora went to the shuttle bay to see the Oonaugh off. The guards were already there, waiting to depart.

Luta tilted, signaling that she would like a private word with Lenora, and they moved slightly away from the others.

"What's wrong? Is everything alright?" Lenora asked.

Luta nodded, her silver eyes unblinking. "I like him. The Verit male. You should keep him."

Lenora was taken aback. In all her years knowing Luta, she had rarely ventured a personal opinion about anything. Certainly never another clan member's relationship status. "Thank you. I do like him.

As for keeping him... I haven't made any decisions yet. I'm not sure if that's even what he wants. The choice isn't only mine, you know."

Luta reached out a hand and placed it a hairsbreadth from her cheek. Lenora felt Luta's energy fill her, still so unlike anything else she had ever encountered. Her energy filled her, gentle and soothing. "The choice is yours, Elle. You know that." She withdrew her energy and patted her cheek gently. "I will give your family your regards."

Lenora nodded a final time, grateful for her support. If one good thing came from this mission, it would be reconnecting with her clan. They were thieves, murderers, and scoundrels, but they were hers.

***

When the time came, it was a ridiculously simple operation. They lay in wait at the appointed coordinates. They set the ship sensors to record, and staged a short, vicious mock battle against the remote-controlled decoy ship, before blowing the empty vessel out of the sky.

They uploaded the recording of proof of vessel destruction to the address listed in the briefing packet and waited for further instruction. It didn't take long. Within just a few hours, they received a simple encoded response:

"Confirmed. Target Destroyed. Payment Transferred."

Immediately, Zera responded. "Thank you. We are interested in further work."

"Noted. No other work needed at this time."

That was it. Nothing more. They stood in silence for a moment before Lenora sighed. "I was afraid of that."

Vordan was incredulous. "That's it? After all that we went through, that's it?"

"They don't know us. We might have to bid on and deliver jobs for months to build up enough reputation to meet someone. This is why the market and the buyer exist, to keep everything anonymous."

"So we're done? We're out?" Vordan couldn't believe it. So much was resting on the success of this mission. The thought that it had all come to nothing made him feel physically sick.

"Not quite."

He turned in surprise to see Scara sitting at one of the analysis terminals. "Excuse me, lady?"

"We are not done. Not yet." Her attention was fixed on the displays floating in front of her, her eyes blinking rapidly as she navigated the menus, and her hands moving invisible keys. "I implanted a tracker in the video. I'm tracing it now. It should tell us who was managing the deal. From there, it will create a backdoor that I can use to snoop around their systems and find the name of the other party."

Vordan couldn't have been more surprised if the Goddess herself appeared and danced naked in front of him. Scara cast a glance at him and burst out laughing at his expression. "Don't look so surprised, Vordan. This is what I do, what I've been trained for. This is how I fight." Her lips quirked at the edges into a self-satisfied smile. "I am an expert in hacking systems and tech espionage. My mother always called it my goddess-gift."

"I didn't know," Vordan replied lamely.

"Why would you? Maman are not in the habit of sharing our secrets with Warriors." The last was said not unkindly. "The trace will take a few hours. Best get some rest. I'll let you know when I get anything."

***

The next morning, they lay in bed snuggling when they were interrupted by a comm from Scara.

"Come now. I'm in, and I have the name of the other party."

They threw on their clothes and raced to the command station, just beating Zera and Odran by seconds. Scara was still sitting at the analysis station, where it appeared she had been all night. She was surrounded by empty drink containers and food wrappers. Gone was her usual Maman poise—her hair was down, her shoes were off, and she was sitting cross-legged in a comfortable reclining chair which Casti had apparently fashioned for her.

Her expression was triumphant. "I've got it! We were right. They are Svobodan."

Vordan whooped and high-fived Odran.

Lenora frowned, considering. "Who is it?"

"Minister Gael. One of their junior senators. He's a key liaison with the Alliance on trade matters."

"Do we have enough evidence?" asked Zera. "Is it enough to take to the Alliance?"

Scara shook her head. "I had to decrypt a lot to get the info. There's no way to copy it from here. It would take an Alliance security expert retracing my steps to see the same connection, and there's no guarantee that they won't find my bug and close the back door between then and now. "

Zera cursed. "So, we are back in the same spot we were before. We know it's Svoboda, but we can't prove it."

"Not necessarily," countered Lenora as she turned to pace the length of the observation room. "You are forgetting about our first stop on this trip. Lucius and Denara are at that medical conference right now. The conference which has Svobodan delegates." She turned to Scara. "If I got you access to a Svobodan ministry log on, would you know what to look for?"

Scara shrugged. "It depends. I know who paid for it, and when, and their codename for the project. The attack at Falosia was 'Operation Olive Branch' and the ongoing attacks on our logistics is 'Operation Black Rock.' I know what to look for, but I have no idea how long it will take me until I get a look at their systems."

"Can you work with Svobodan systems?" asked Zera.

Scara looked at her archly. "Who else would I be training to hack? Verit has long believed Svoboda was responsible for our current situation. We have been in a cold war for years. Much of my training was aimed at getting into Svobodan systems."

"Alright. New plan." Lenora took a deep breath. "We are going to that conference. We'll steal the access of a high ranking Svobodan official and get the evidence we need." She turned to Zera. "Please comm Denara and Lucius and give them the heads up that we are coming. Scara, can you hack the conference systems and issue us delegate passes?"

"No problem at all."

"Actually, can you issue other passes?" asked Odran.

"Like what?"

"Cleaning, maintenance, security..."

Lenora's eyes lit up. "That's brilliant. We could go anywhere without interruption. It's likely that they've brought in extra help for the conference. They would expect unfamiliar faces."

"Done." Scara nodded.

Chapter Fourteen

The Heist

They met Denara and Lucius in the lobby of the conference hotel for drinks. The conference was held in a hotel in a major transport hub. In addition to the hundreds of conference guests, there were thousands of people trafficking through every day, many of them opting to pop into the hotel for a bite to eat, a drink at the bar, or a quick twelve-hour nap and a freshen up. All around them, lots of business meetings were happening in the large lobby café. As a result, the hotel had helpfully installed privacy fields. When activated, no one outside of the table could hear what was being discussed. The café was in a modern style, filled with natural light filtering in from the large plate window walls, reflecting off polished floor tiles and glass tables. Plush rugs and large plants were interspersed around the room, alleviating the coldness of all the hard surfaces.

Denara and Lucius had been busy gathering intel. There were several high ranking Svobodan officials that they could target in attendance. They settled on Minister Obana, the minister for finance and international trade. If anyone officially sanctioned paying mercenaries, they figured he would know about it.

Lenora laid out the plan. "The Minister has been assigned both personal rooms and an office while he is at the conference. Scara has issued us passes and inserted us into the staff roster as new hires from a contract agency, brought in for the conference. Scara and Zera will pose as maintenance techs. They will go to the tech hub and access the security protocols and cameras to upgrade our pass access to full clearance and deactivate the cameras to cover our tracks, then evac to Casti." Scara looked scared, but Zera nodded firmly. Lenora smiled at her; she knew Zera would protect the young Maman at all costs.

"Vordan and Odran have been assigned security passes. They will create a distraction by contacting the Minister and letting him know that there has been a security breach–someone has turned off the cameras in his office rooms. They will attend to inspect them and require his presence to verify that nothing has been taken or accessed." The males nodded in unison.

"I have been assigned a cleaning pass. I will gain access to the Minister's personal rooms as a cleaner. I will wait until he and most of his staff are dealing with the security issue and plant a bug that Scara has prepared for us. Once connected to his access devices, it will bypass his security and give her free rein to inspect the ministry files."

Scara spoke. "I have actually prepared two. Vordan and Odran will have one as well, just in case his device is in his office rather than his personal rooms."

Lenora took a deep breath. "There's lots that might go wrong with this. These operations usually take weeks of planning, but the conference only lasts for another few days. The Minister might not fall for the bait, he might keep his access devices on him personally, he may leave security behind in his offices, someone might find Scara's hack, the files may not be on ministry servers…" She stopped herself. "What

I'm saying is that we need to be careful and ready to adapt to whatever happens."

Vordan smiled gently at her and squeezed her hand. "Don't worry so much. We've worked it out so far."

She took another calming breath. "Alright. The conference will be in recess this afternoon. There's no formal dinner. We will aim for 1600, just before the end of the day. Scara, make sure we are all rostered on."

That decided, they ordered a meal and drinks, simply relaxing before what was to come. Lenora felt herself slowly unclench, as she enjoyed the camaraderie of the others. Repeatedly she felt Denara's gaze stray to herself and Vordan, so she was expecting the question when it came.

"So forgive me for being nosey... but when did this happen?" She waved her fork between them. "It's adorable."

Lenora went bright red, and Vordan did a wonderful impression of a stunned creature in headlights. She cleared her throat and mumbled a reply. "It's, um, it's new."

"I see," was Denara's mischievous reply.

"I think it's adorable," piped Scara, and Vordan nearly wrenched his neck, looking at her in shock. He swallowed twice before he could reply.

"Thank you, Maman." Belatedly Lenora realized how much a Maman's approval of their relationship would mean to him. Despite being a Junior Maman, males on Verit were heavily conditioned to desire their approbation. Her words touched something deep in him. Lenora reached over and patted his knee, and he clamped his hand down on hers.

"Alright, enough embarrassing them," grumbled Lucius. "Let's all take a break before tonight."

"We have to report for work and get our uniforms at 1400," Scara informed them. "We have a couple of hours."

***

Lenora and Vordan said their goodbyes and wandered outside. The hotel was in the middle of a sprawling modern metropolis. All around them were glass buildings, fabricated in a variety of unusual shapes. In between the buildings, and crawling up their walls, were gardens of every conceivable color and design. The Haven colony leaders had learned from other, less successful colonies, and had been determined that their planetary development would not result in a damaged eco-system. The result was large high-tech cities that appeared to grow out of the greenery.

They wandered paths that wound around, and sometimes through, the buildings, scenting the clean air filled with smells of growing things. Eventually, they reached an open square filled with office workers gathering for lunch. Several enterprising food vendors had set up outside tables and floating service carts.

Vordan watched Lenora look longingly at one of the carts. "What is it?"

"It's an old-Earth delicacy. It's flavored ice, covered in fruit. My father used to get it for us when we were little." Eating the flavored ice with her sister and her father was one of her best childhood memories.

"Would you like some?"

Her eyes lit up. "Yes!" They wandered over and took their time selecting the flavors and fruits. The end result was a ridiculous, sticky, sugary mess that she tucked into with abandon. They sat in the sunshine, reflected on the glass buildings, under the shade of the creeping gardens. It was beautiful.

It could be like this, he realized. After their mission, assuming that he could convince the Maman to let him mate with her, it could be like this. They could travel on missions together, exploring the galaxy. There would be adventure, interspersed with time for them.

He could still feel their bond, quiet now but ever-present. It had grown stronger over the past few days until it felt like breathing. Verit were not psychic, but he could swear he could reach out and touch it, touch her with his mind. So he did. In his mind, he imagined reaching out a hand and stroking back her mane of hair.

He wasn't sure what reaction he had been expecting, but for Lenora to yelp and nearly drop her ice wasn't it. She whipped around to look at him, her eyes wide like saucers. "You touched the bond!" Her voice was hushed, awed. "You aren't meant to be able to do that!"

He shrugged. "I didn't know that." He examined her flushed face. "What did it feel like?"

She smiled at him mischievously. He waited, expectantly, and cursed when he felt her fingers curl around his penis, stroking gently. "Lenora!" he breathed, his eyes darting around them at the oblivious office workers eating lunch.

"That's what it feels like." She ginned wider, and he felt nails scraping down his inner thighs, along with a phantom tongue that disappeared just as it hit his groin.

"You are wicked, lady." He concentrated, imagining kissing her, imagining lapping at her, teasing with his teeth.

She reached out and grabbed his thigh, sinking her nails in. "Ok, truce. Again with the public places!"

He chuckled darkly. "I like this. It has lots of possibilities."

"The bond is getting stronger," she responded. "Are you still ok with it?"

He nodded, stealing a lick of her flavored ice. He considered his response, how much to say. He could hedge his bets... but it wasn't in his nature. Honesty and loyalty were the core of him. He looked at her. "I love you, Lenora. I know it's fast and crazy, but I do." She was stunned. "I know that the timing is bad. You don't need to do anything about it. But I wanted you to know. This mission is risky. Anything could happen. Before we go in there, I want you to know that I love you. When this is over, promise me we'll take the time to see how we feel."

Lenora opened her mouth to speak. He could sense her uncertainty. "You don't have to say anything. I just wanted you to know. We'll work the rest out after."

Lenora looked at him for a long moment, judging his sincerity. He felt her probing the bond, feeling his emotions. Eventually she nodded and took another lick of her ice. They sat there in quiet, companionable silence together, just watching the world go by for a few minutes. He could feel her working through her thoughts.

Eventually, she spoke. "Vordan?"

"Yeah?"

She turned to look at him, and he was struck again by how beautiful she was. Her pale skin and wild hair. She looked like a queen from an ancient tale. "I love you too. I don't know what the hell to do about it right now, but I do. I promise, when this is over, we'll work it out. But I can't focus on this just now. The mission has to come first. Over everything. Even this." She braced, waiting for his reaction.

He smiled and snagged his arm around her waist, pulling her snugly into him. "I know, lady. You wouldn't be the female I love if you felt any different."

He felt some of her tension leave her. They sat together for a little longer. "Want another ice?" she asked.

Chapter Fifteen

Sneaky

The plan fell apart almost immediately. Lenora watched the males and Zera and Scara register, get their passes and uniforms, and head in their respective directions. She waited her assigned fifteen minutes and walked up to the registration desk for the staff to clock in. She picked up her badge and uniform and was directed to an older female. She was short, squat, dark purple with fierce orange facial feathers and a no-nonsense attitude.

"Good afternoon. I am Shalu. I am floor supervisor for housekeeping on the ranking delegate floor." She squinted at Lenora. "Have you worked here before?"

"No, this is my first time."

Shalu harrumphed. "What are they doing? Assigning a newbie to the delegate floor. New personnel aren't allowed to work with VIPs without at least two months of training and experience. Goddam new admin people don't know what they are doing. Wait here, I'll need to get you swapped with one of the regulars."

"No, it's alright." Lenora cut in hastily, lying through her teeth. "I have extensive experience in other hotels, that's probably why. They said they were really short staffed today."

Shalu squinted at her again considering, one fang chewing at her lip. Finally, she grunted. "I don't have time for this. Ok, stick by me. Do exactly as I say; don't speak to anyone and don't go anywhere without me. Got it?"

Lenora meekly responded, "Yes, Shalu."

Lenora followed her up through the bowels of the hotel service areas, into the goods elevator, to the delegate floor. They entered the long delegate corridor. Dark red wood paneling on the walls, plush creamy rugs on the floors, and ornate plaster ceilings. It screamed old world money, taste, and refinement. The doors were dark red enamel, set wide apart, with discrete numbers to the side and a little doorbell on each.

Shalu stopped at the first door and motioned for her to wait. Lenora smiled at her politely, thankful that Scara had given her the room number of Minister Obana. At the other end of the corridor, she saw a hulking male in a black body suit step out of the room and look them up and down before nodding and ducking back inside.

With delegates on this floor, every room probably had their own security personnel. She would have to be very careful. They proceeded to clean the first few rooms. Shalu gave her a checklist to work through and hissed at her approximately every five minutes when she failed to clean to her exacting standards or moved a fraction too slowly.

It was mind-numbing, backbreaking work. Apparently, this hotel didn't believe in modern cleaning bots. Lenora silently promised herself that she would never take cleaning personnel for granted again. The one benefit of working through the other rooms was that each suite had a similar layout. A large open lounge/dining/ kitchenette area, with two bedrooms off to one side, both with ensuite bathrooms, and a large office area on the other side of the open area. Like the corridor, everything was tasteful in shades of red, cream, and brown.

The furniture was antique, dotted with high tech appliances here and there.

Lenora begrudgingly admitted that the interior design was genius—it practically screamed money and comfort, with nothing to prove.

At the agreed time for the distraction, she waited for the call on her HUD. It came like clockwork.

"Cameras disabled," reported Scara.

"Security dispatched," responded Vordan. "On our way now." She waited in anticipation for several more minutes. "Minister Obana has been contacted."

"Cameras show he is on his way," responded Scara. "Lenora, go now. Maintenance team is evacuating to Casti."

Lenora moved towards a small bar in the dining area and picked up a glass, which she purposely bobbled and dropped. Shalu whirled around to her, hissing her displeasure. Lenora bent to pick it up and sliced her finger on a sharp shard, purposefully smearing the blood around to make the cut look bigger.

"Oh, damn it. I need to go get medical attention. I've cut myself."

Instantly Shalu's demeanor changed, and she hustled over, clucking at her. "That's nasty. Come on, I'll show you where medical is."

"No, it's fine. I know I haven't been much help today. I don't want to put you further behind. Just tell me where to go."

Shalu's mouth firmed. "No, you'll never find it. Employee medical is down in the service area. I'll take you there and come straight back. It won't take more than ten minutes. They'll patch you up straight away, they have a skin regen—you'll be in and out and back at work in no time."

Not seeing any other option, Lenora smiled gratefully. When Shalu turned back to her trolley, Lenora reached into the pocket of her uniform and produced a stunner, which she applied to the back of Shalu's neck. The other women went down straight away. Lenora caught her and dragged her into a closet in the bedroom, grabbing the access card from her belt.

"My apologies, Shalu. But it's better this way. I don't want them blaming you for this."

Returning to the main area, Lenora quickly wrapped her wound with a small emergency Med Patch from her kit and grabbed the trolley. She confidently walked up the corridor and tapped on the Minister's door, saying, "Housekeeping."

She waited. After a minute or so, she swiped the access card and entered the room. She hurried to the office, where the Minister's secondary portable secure connection was set up. Like most people, he used some form of HUD and connected to whatever wireless display was available when he didn't want it to overlay his vision. Unlike most people though, he was accessing highly sensitive material, so used a portable secure connection point to encrypt his HUD transmissions.

His main one would be in the office, where the males were with him now, but this secondary one was common. She palmed the bug that Scara had given her and held it up to the side of the security hub. The hub was a small opalescent sphere sitting on the desk. Scara's bug appeared like a flat piece of metal.

Lenora placed the bug next to the sphere, and it began to transform. Fine tendrils of the metal extended and probed the surface of the sphere, wrapping the tendrils round and round until the surface of the sphere was crisscrossed in a fine metal web. It stilled for a moment, flashing bright white, before it sunk into the sphere. The sphere returned to its normal opalescent state.

Lenora comm'd Scara. "Bug attached."

"Connecting now," came the immediate response. "I'm in. This is going to take time; the security is very complex."

"How long?"

"I don't know. Perhaps a couple of hours."

Lenora sighed and comm'd Vordan. "I need you to stall as long as you can."

It took a couple of minutes before he could respond. "Acknowledged, will do."

She looked around the room, debating her options. She needed to hide their tracks. Distraction was still their best strategy. Decided, she set about methodically rummaging through the room. She tried to make it look like she was looking for something. Basic psychology–if they thought she was a thief, they would be more focused on what was missing, rather than what had been added.

Ten minutes later, she stood in the apartment that had been turned over. Closets and drawers were open, items moved around. She had grabbed several expensive looking jewelry items as justification. She couldn't do any more than she had. It was time to make her own exit before Shalu woke up, or she was discovered.

Lenora grabbed the trolley, stuffing her stolen items under some linen, and exited the room, walking down the corridor. As she walked down the corridor, the male from the other room opened the door again.

He saw her, nodded politely, and began to go back into his room before he stopped. "Where is the other one?"

"Excuse me?" she asked, her heart pounding.

"Where is the other housekeeper?"

"Oh, she needed more supplies, so she went to get them."

He frowned. "No, she didn't. No other hotel staff apart from you have been in this corridor in the past hour." Lenora smiled and shrugged and turned to continue. "Wait, show me your identification."

She pulled her staff ID, cursing the unusually efficient guard. The identity Scara had created for them would not stand up to any scrutiny. He scanned it, nodding when it flashed green in confirmation that she was authorized to be on the floor.

"Can I go now? I have more rooms to do."

He levelled a steely gaze at her. "Why did you skip rooms?"

"Sorry?"

"Why did you skip rooms? You were in that room down there, then you skipped to the Svobodan Minister one. Why did you skip those rooms?"

"I'm sorry, I don't know. I just cleaned the rooms I was assigned."

He frowned. "You're lying." He straightened and grabbed her arm.

"Let me go, you're hurting me!" she squirmed, feigning fear.

"I am Head of VIP Security here at the hotel. I'm taking you into custody. Stop resisting. You won't be harmed if you cooperate."

She let herself go slack, and he stumbled slightly at her unexpected weight. It was all the opening she needed. She swiped a low kick that took his legs out from under him and twisted her arm away. She took off in a sprint towards the stairs. "I've been spotted. Heading down the north stairs. Everyone evac now. Do not assist."

"Hey!" she heard him shout and curse behind her, and comm for help.

She hit the stairwell door, slamming through it and took the stairs three at a time. They were on the tenth floor–it was unlikely that she would be able to escape. With this many VIPs, there would be security on every floor. They would corner her. The entire plan had relied on secrecy.

They caught her as she passed the eighth floor. She heard motion behind her, and a searing agony short circuited her muscles. She crumpled, falling down the stairs headfirst. She was dimly aware of a crack and more searing pain in her wrist, and of her face burning as she scraped it against the wall before she blacked out.

***

Vordan stumbled, clutching his chest. He leaned against the wall outside the Minister's public offices, hiding the searing pain that blew through him. They had extricated themselves on Lenora's orders and were moving to meet at the rendezvous point.

It took only a second to realize what had happened. He looked at Odran, murmuring sub-vocally, "They've got her."

Odran's eyes widened a fraction before he regained focus, his gaze sharpening. The stark fear that filled Vordan was the worst thing he had ever experienced. It was a yawning pit of darkness that threatened to swallow him fully. Within it was an icy rage that nipped at him with serrated teeth.

His love, his mate, was captured. Seriously injured if the pain was any indication. There was no way that he could leave her behind, whatever her orders.

He surrendered to the darkness. His people called it the Dark Stranger, the darkness within. The generically imprinted rage that made them such vicious fighters that generations past Maman had bred into them to save their face. He welcomed it, embraced the darkness as a friend. It numbed him, bringing everything into sharp focus.

Scara comm'd him. Her voice was low, shaky. "They've captured Lenora. She's down. They are taking her to the holding cells in the basement."

He straightened, pushing away the echoes of Lenora's pain. "Send me the map. How do I get there?"

"She said not to assist her."

"I don't care. Send me the map."

"Vordan-" Her voice was reluctant.

"She's my mate, Scara. I cannot leave her."

There was a long pause before Zera came on the comm. "We're sending you the details... Fuck orders, Vordan. Bring my sister back."

"Yes, lady. Finish the mission, complete the hack. I'll get Lenora."

"We will," she promised.

The map data streamed into his HUD.

"Are you coming, Odran?"

Odran looked at him like he was an idiot. "I can't believe you'd even ask."

He nodded. His brothers would never abandon his mate, either. Nothing would stand in his way of recovering his love. He simply couldn't imagine life without her. She was so cool, smart, strong. He had never imagined that the Goddess would bless him with a mate like her, and he'd be damned if some Svobodan bastard would take her.

Chapter Sixteen

Interrogation

L enora woke to a world of agony. Every nerve was on fire, the pain creating a nausea trying to crawl its way up her throat. Her vision was fuzzy, but gradually she became aware of her surroundings. She was in a gray room, lying on a solid bed that extruded from the gray wall. There was a table and chair in the room, both bolted to the ground, and a toilet and sink in the corner. She'd been in enough jail cells the galaxy over to recognize one.

They must have hit her with a neuro tranq. It was the only thing she knew of that would cause instant loss of nerve and muscle control, and which left the victim in agony for days. She swallowed; her throat was parched. Some cheaper neuro tranqs also caused permanent neurological damage. It was why they were outlawed on most planets.

Well, there's nothing to be done about that now. Whatever damage there would be was already done. She tried to lever herself up on her side and screamed when she put weight on her wrist and flopped back down. *Ok, wrist broken too.* She took stock. Her weapons were gone, HUD gone. She wore just her black jumpsuit and her bare feet. At least they had let her keep the jumpsuit. It would provide some basic first aid for her.

A door opened in the opposite wall and two males walked in. They wore jumpsuits and long robes–they were Svobodan. She swallowed.

"It's about time you were awake. We've been waiting patiently to have a little chat with you."

She tried to speak and managed only the barest whisper. "Then you shouldn't have stunned me."

One of them barked out a laugh, while the other's lips thinned to a fine line at her impudence. The one that had laughed went to the door and whispered something, returning a moment later with a glass of water and a straw, which he held up to her to drink from.

She was pathetically weak but couldn't risk refusing the water even if he had laced it with something. She tentatively sipped until she had finished it.

"There now. Let's help you up and have a chat." He assisted her to sit up, his touch lingering a little too long to be impersonal. When she winced in pain at the moment of her wrist, she sensed a flash of satisfaction. It chilled her. This male delighted in the pain of others. He would hurt her, simply because he could, and he enjoyed it.

He helped her to move to the chair at the table while the other male watched dispassionately.

"Who are you?" the other male asked.

"Surely you've checked my ID by now."

"We have. We know what it says. But who are you really?"

"I'm a housekeeper. I just started today."

The dangerous male spoke again, his voice gentle and chiding, like she was a misbehaving child. She suspected many people had been fooled by that voice. "A housekeeper with a state-of-the-art Falosian jumpsuit, that managed to turn off security cameras, to engineer a distraction to break into a Svobodan Minister's room just to steal some jewelry?"

She looked him in the eye. "Yes."

He laughed softly, his kind eyes disappointed in her. "Please don't do this the hard way. We don't want to harm you." *Please do this the hard way,* his mind whispered, and her stomach lurched at the rotting perversion she sensed there.

The other male tsked in displeasure. "We will find out. No one attacks a Svobodan Minister and gets away with it. Tell us who you are, who you are working for, and what you want!"

She stiffened. "I am a housekeeper. I started today. I saw the jewelry and took it."

"Very well." He turned to the dangerous one. "It seems your skills will be needed after all, my friend."

The dangerous male went to the door again and returned with a rolled-up piece of material. He methodically unrolled it to display a set of instruments. He selected the first one, a long thin dull black probe, and pressed it against her forearm. She tried to move away, but the other male clamped her broken wrist to the table. She screamed in pain as a crawling heat began moving through her, like tiny bites of fire. She realized she couldn't move anything below her neck at all.

"This is a useful device. You will be unable to move, but you can still feel." He smiled gently at her again. "It will also prevent you from falling unconscious."

He settled back and picked up another tool. He swiped it across her hand, and the skin split precisely, revealing muscle. "Tell me who you are."

"I am a housekeeper."

He placed a precise split next to the first one and she grit her teeth as he watched the red blood bead and trickle down her skin. "Tell me who you are," he whispered, caressing her cheek with a finger.

She took a deep breath. She needed to stall, to give Scara time to finish her hack. "I am a housekeeper."

***

They spent several minutes considering their options. In their security uniforms, they only had small side arm pistols and stunners. It was insufficient to take on a larger force, so Vordan and Odran went first to the security office. They needed weapons, and the in-house security team had them. They walked right in, their passes still active, and stunned the two males on duty within ten seconds.

They wasted more precious time opening the armory. When they finally got through the security protecting it, Vordan whistled in appreciation. There was enough gear to take a small military base. The arms lined the wall in a precision that Lenora would have been proud of. After a quick glance around, they took a selection of pulse rifles, explosives, and a range of other toys. They put on body armor, and Odran grabbed a heavy-duty med kit backpack. Vordan growled when he saw it but said nothing.

The holding cells were two levels down. As soon as they left the security office, they would be exposed. It was only a matter of time before they were spotted. They trotted down the corridor, falling into a standard search pattern. Vordan took the lead, Odran backup. The first person they encountered was a maintenance tech, who took one look at them loping along with their armor and guns and immediately ducked back into the doorway he had come from, and slammed it shut.

They encountered several housekeeping staff, who ran in the opposite direction. Another minute passed, and they reached the stairwell to take them down to the cells. The sirens blared to life around them. "Security Alert! Security Alert! Basement Level three, all security personnel. Lockdown initiated."

Vordan cursed and threw open the stairwell door before it could lock, and they flew down the two flights of stairs to reach the cell level. As expected, it had locked with the security protocol.

Vordan pulled the explosives from the backpack, and began applying them to the doorframe, while above them, he could hear the sounds of the security force making its way down to them from the upper levels.

***

Lenora floated on the pain, its razor cotton candy filling her mind, making it hard to think. Her left arm was filled with precise cuts that dribbled blood, and he had started on her right. She promised herself that before she was done here, she would kill the bastard so that he would never torture anyone else. Even if it was the last thing she did.

She had to admit, though, that she wasn't doing well. The nerve tranq had done actual damage, and her nerves were shorting randomly. Her wrist was black and swollen, and the blood dribbling from her wounds had started to slow; she was bleeding out.

There was a discrete knock at the door, and the other male went to it. He came back, satisfaction writ on his face.

"Madame Oonaugh. What a pleasure. We had thought you were long dead."

She bared her teeth at him. "Well done, you win a prize. Took you long enough."

"Madame Oonaugh, we both know you don't stoop to anything as ordinary as jewelry theft. What were you doing in the Minister's rooms?"

She raised her chin, the only part of her body that she could move, in defiance and remained silent.

The dangerous male jumped when the lights flickered, red emergency lights coming on and an automated security alert ringing out. He moved to the door again and had another whispered conversation.

"It seems you weren't working alone, Madame Oonaugh. We must accelerate this conversation."

Lenora blanked for a moment before her brain caught up with his words. She knew immediately what was happening. Vordan would come for her. It simply wasn't part of his make-up to leave her behind. In all her life, she had never met anyone as loyal as him. Plus, he loved her. She still couldn't quite wrap her head around that. It seemed impossible and improbable, but it was true. She reached for him with her empathy, feeling him nearby, his mind swirling with a cold, dark rage, and bone-chilling fear for her.

The dangerous male reached out and slapped her, and she refocused her eyes on him. "Pay attention, Madame Oonaugh." He hissed, and she saw real fury glittering in his eyes. He didn't like her ignoring him.

"But you are boring me, dear. There are only so many times I can listen to you ask the same question. Is the art of conversation dead on Svoboda?"

He snarled and plucked a long knife from the roll and slammed it into her thigh. She let out a short shriek, the pain strangling the sound in her throat.

"Oh, my," he said mildly. "Look what you made me do. I've nicked your femoral artery. We can't have you bleeding out." He took a tourniquet from the pack and wrapped it around her leg. "We have so much more to discuss. I promise I shall try to be more interesting."

The other male tapped him on the shoulder. "No time for games now. This needs to be sped up. Use it."

The dangerous one pouted, reluctant. "It's risky. We could lose her."

The other one persisted. "It's a risk I'll take. Do it."

Dangerous nodded and took a small vial from the roll. He delicately placed two droplets from the vial into one of her wounds, and she froze. It was warm, calming. It rolled through her like honey, heating her insides and relaxing her. She knew what this was. *Egia*, truth serum. It relaxed its subject, made them highly susceptible to suggestion.

She clamped her jaw shut and went deep inside her mind. This was no longer about stalling; it was about loyalty. She knew too many secrets, could not afford to have them exposed to Svoboda. There was danger to empathy. It was too easy to empathize with others, to be pulled into their feelings and emotions. Most Falosian hospitals had a ward where there were empaths that had gone too deep and become lost. She reached for Vordan, for his mind, and submerged herself. She would rather spend her last minutes deep in his memories of her, protecting her people's secrets, than here in this room with these two butchers. *I'm sorry, my love. I wanted that future with you, but I can't let them have our secrets.*

***

Vordan blew the door, risking being shot to poke his head around the doorway. He turned to Odran. "Five left in the hallway. Three down."

Odran nodded, his attention on the stairs. "Two security teams coming down. Less than one minute." He cocked his head, listening intently. "Eight security officers, at least."

Vordan considered. "We need to get into that hallway. It's more defensible than this stairwell."

He threw a grenade into the hallway, waiting a split second after it detonated before Odran and he burst through the doorway, shooting the remaining personnel. They raced down the corridor, turning right where the HUD map showed Lenora was being held. He didn't need the map anymore. He could feel her. Feel her pain and anger. She felt strangely close, closer than she had ever been in their intimate moments before. With a jolt, he realized that she had connected to him empathically.

He stopped outside the doorway where she was being held and reached with his mind, stretching for her. *How many, my queen?*

He felt her trying to reply, her mind sluggish, and he squashed the fear that welled up at how weak her mental voice was. *Two,* she whispered back, giving him impressions of them. One disgusted her, while the other was a still, quiet figure.

He motioned to Odran that there were two, and they burst through the door. One male stood before a desk. On it was a roll with bloody instruments.

The other leapt around behind Lenora, who was tied to a metal chair. Vordan roared when he saw her; she was bruised and bloodied, dozens of cuts marring her arms and face. She lolled limply. They had tied her because she was unable to hold herself up. The male behind her gripped her neck.

"Come any closer and I'll break her neck," he ordered, his voice clipped.

He felt Lenora gathering herself. *Be ready*, she whispered. He didn't get a chance to ask, before the male gripping her screamed, tearing at his own arms and eyes. The other male stood frozen in shock, and Vordan reached out with his hand, unsheathed his claws, and raked him across his face.

The male shrieked in pain, and Vordan backhanded him contemptuously. The male bounced against a bunk protruding from the wall, scrambling to get away, blinded by the cuts to his eyes. Vordan fell on him like a monster. He dug his claws into his stomach through his robes and hauled out his intestines. He roared, biting through his neck, delighting in watching the male's life drain out of his face with his blood.

"Vordan!" called Odran. He spun around, ready to fight, but instead saw Odran untying Lenora, the other male lying motionless on the floor. He helped Odran lay her on the bunk as Odran frantically examined her.

"She needs immediate medical assistance. She's dying." Odran's voice was grim.

"Lenora, love. We have you. You're safe." Vordan touched her cheek, one of the few places on her that wasn't damaged. Her eyes flickered, but she didn't open them. He heard her voice whisper in his head. *I got him, that bastard. Won't hurt anyone else.*

Yes, you did, he replied. *Come back, love.*

Can't. She mumbled, *used everything left for the empathic push to kill him. Love you, Vordan. Thank you for being mine, just for a little while.*

Odran stilled and began chest compressions. "Her heart has stopped. She needs help now!"

"Tell me what to do!" He grabbed the MedBag Odran had brought.

"Nothing in there will help her. She needs the medical facility on Casti."

Vordan snapped. "That isn't much help now—we need to fight our way back out!"

Odran stopped compressions and Vordan snarled at him. Odran spoke to him sub-vocally. "There is a way. We can teleport."

"WHAT?"

"Casti has teleport capability. But if we use it... everyone will know. There's no way to hide it. There are cameras in here. No other species has the tech already. It'll scream that we have alien tech. There will be no more hiding."

Vordan stilled. This was a huge decision. He wanted to save Lenora, but to do so would expose the entire colony. "What do Zera and Scara say?"

Odran paused, communicating with Zera. He refocused. "They say do it."

Vordan sucked in a deep breath. "Alright, do it."

The world disappeared in front of him into a million sparks.

Chapter Seventeen

Healing and Love

Vordan sat by her bedside in the medical bay, watching her chest rise and fall.

Casti had transported them straight into the MedBay, and immediately immersed Lenora into a healing pod full of a viscous dark fluid. He hadn't seen her in hours. After the adrenaline of the fight, he had been left shaky and empty. His mind kept replaying her last words to him, praying that they wouldn't be her last words ever.

He checked in on Scara and Zera, who had made their evac with no issues. Scara had completed the hack. She was still working her way through the files she had copied, but she said that she already had enough evidence that the Svobodans had paid for the attacks on the colony. It was enough to take to the Alliance. It was cold comfort.

He had eventually found himself back in MedBay, where Casti had thoughtfully provided him with a chair to sit in. He must have fallen asleep, because when he awoke, she was lying there in a MedBay beside him. Deeply asleep, but alive.

Her arms bore the tracery of the little cuts in pink, already healing and fading, and her wrist appeared whole again. He blinked. It was like a dream; he couldn't believe it.

He could feel her again, in his mind, banked like fire. He reached over and smoothed the wildness of her hair back and pressed a trembling kiss to her forehead.

"Don't do that to me again, Pirate Queen. I don't think my heart could take it."

"I'll try not to, Flyboy," she murmured sleepily. His eyes jumped to hers. She looked at him through heavy lids, half awake. "Shh. Talk more in the morning." She rolled over, cupping his arm to her, and fell asleep. Chuckling, he allowed himself to be pulled into bed with her and curled himself protectively around her. He lay there for hours, watching her sleep, content in her presence. He promised himself that whatever happened, he would never allow her to be harmed again. If he had to glue himself to her damned side forever, he'd do so.

***

In the morning, reality intruded once more. Scara had completed her analysis, and they were summoned home. It was funny how quickly the colony had become home. It seemed surreal. Just weeks ago, Vordan and Lenora had been sitting in the K'Dec's office, receiving their orders. They were there again, but so much had changed.

Lenora sat next to Vordan, weak, pale, but upright. She had a spine of steel, and he was beyond proud of her. Across from her was the K'Dec, G'Dec Sraya, the Senior Maman Frei and Scara. Next to her, Odran and Zera completed the table.

"Report," she commanded.

Lenora took a deep breath and did just that. She recounted their time with the Oonaugh, the farce at the market, the auction, destroying the decoy and then their disastrous last mission which had nearly cost her life.

The K'Dec sat silently once her report was over, considering, before she turned to Scara. "What did you find?"

"Enough evidence to conclusively tie Svoboda to the sabotage attempts. Payments, instructions, plans. It was a government sanctioned project, with several other Ministers involved."

The K'Dec looked at the Maman. Frei smiled viciously. "Let's do it. We needed the evidence. We have it. Put the plan into action."

The K'Dec held up a finger to stall her. "What about our other questions? Is this part of a greater plan, and what is the end goal? Are they aware that we have Zyilan and ancient tech on this planet?"

Scara nodded. "Yes. They know. They landed an operative here months before we got here, who reported it back. It's why they have been trying to sabotage us. At first, it was simple misogyny. They just wanted to make sure there were no more matriarchal societies established. But when they found the Zyilan, their priorities changed. They wanted it for themselves. It would give them unmatched power in the Alliance. If they can't get it for themselves, they want to make sure we can't have it."

The Maman snarled, her white canines exposed. The K'Dec nodded once and stood. "Thank you, all of you, for everything you have done. Scara, debrief in detail with G'Dec Sraya. Lenora, if I may have a moment?"

The others stood and made their exits. Vordan lingered for a moment, catching Lenora's eye. She gave him a nod of reassurance and he left.

"How are you, Lenora?" The K'Dec came to sit next to her, concern in her yellow eyes. "Really?"

"Tired, Maral. I'm exhausted. Mentally, emotionally, physically. I'm burned out."

"I heard what you didn't say in the briefing. I know how you killed that male. You emanated."

Lenora shrugged. "He was an evil male. I made him remember everything he had ever done. Made him feel it." She bared her teeth. "I knew it would kill me—I've never been a strong empath. It took everything I had left. But it was worth it to take him out of this world, to leave it safer."

"I'm so sorry I had to ask you to do this again. I promise, it's the last time."

Lenora sighed. "Don't make promises you can't keep. If Falosia needs us, you know I'll do it again." She smiled crookedly. "It wasn't all bad. I got to reconnect with my family. And I had tried too hard to bury Elle. I forgot the fun parts of being her. She worried a lot less about everything. It was kind of freeing, actually. Forget the rule book and do whatever I thought best."

Maral smiled. "And Vordan. Every empath in the colony can feel your connection. It's blazing."

Lenora's grin widened. "And the flyboy." She paused, overcome with emotion. "HE is the best thing that's ever happened to me." She gripped her friend's hand. "If I had to do this a hundred times over, to meet him, I'd do it. He's worth it."

Maral held her back just as tightly. "I'm so happy for you, and so glad to see the real you again, my friend. It's been too long. You were so keen to bury Elle, but it was Elle's fire and spirit that I met in the bar that night. I worried that we'd buried you forever."

The K'Dec sat back and blinked wet eyes. "As for what happens now, I have a proposal for you."

"Oh? Not an order."

"No. Not an order. You've earned the right to choose. If you want to, you can stay here. Run logistics, build your home."

"But?"

"The L'Kar and the Matriarch have met in secret and put a plan in motion for when we had evidence. They will jointly confront the Alliance about Svoboda's treachery. If the Alliance won't take action, Verit, Falosia, and all their colonies will secede from the Alliance and form our own group."

"You can't be serious... that's somewhat drastic."

"It is. And we hope it won't come to that. But if Svoboda isn't stopped here, if the Alliance won't draw a line in the sand, it will be the same as giving them free rein to do as they please." The K'Dec smirked. "Besides, we have contingencies in place. The Alliance controls most of the Zyilan in this part of the galaxy. It is extremely difficult for non-human species to buy in any quantity, given how xenophobic the Alliance is. What we have on this planet is ten times what the Alliance has. We have made a deal with the Maluriens, and a couple of others. We will become a trading planet for aliens wishing to buy Zyilan, and a research station for alien tech. In exchange for them applying economic, political, and martial pressure on the Alliance."

Lenora gaped. This was so far beyond what she had imagined... it was incredibly ambitious. A huge gamble beyond anything attempted in human interstellar politics thus far.

"What does this mean for me?

"We have been researching the data from Casti, and believe we know where there may be other ancient alien ships and tech. I want you to lead a team to locate them. Bring them back here."

Lenora considered it for a split second before she laughed outright, delight bubbling through her. "Can I bring the flyboy?"

It was perfect. Everything she could have ever wanted, if she had been brave enough to imagine for herself such a wild fire life. It gave her the freedom to explore, away from the rules and confines that had become too small for her, would feed her newfound joy of adventure, but still enabled her to help her people.

Maral laughed. "Who else is going to fly your ship?"

***

Vordan paced anxiously outside the K'Dec's office, waiting to assist Lenora back to bed. Spine of steel or not, the female should be resting. He stopped mid-step when he felt the sharp spike of joy in her, his lips lifting at the corners in echo. Whatever it was, his queen was delighted.

She limped out of the door just a few minutes later, and he moved to offer her his arm, supporting her as she walked. "Can we sit in the sunshine on the green?" she asked.

He changed direction and led them to a comfy patch in full sunlight, away from the mess hall and the prying eyes and ears, keen to enquire about their trip.

She turned to him, the sun playing through those wild black curls of hers. "I love you, you know? With everything in me. I knew you would come for me."

Her blunt statement took his breath away. So did the look in her clear eyes. There was an open honesty that he had rarely seen in another living creature. "I love you too, Pirate Queen. I thought I would die when I saw you. Please, do not ask me to watch that again. I don't think my heart could take it."

She leaned forward and pressed a gentle kiss to his lips. "I have a question for you."

"Yes?" he replied instantly.

She laughed and whacked him gently. "This is serious. You don't even know what I'm asking."

"I am serious. Whatever you wish, if it is within my power to give it to you, I will. You are my Pirate Queen, and you have stolen my heart and soul."

"Vordan..." Her mouth hung open in shock. "That's beautiful."

She sniffed and blinked back tears, leaning in to kiss him again.

"But you must listen. The K'Dec has given me a new mission."

He started. "What!?" She was barely healed from the last!

"Hush. Just listen." She explained their new mission. "You will be away from your brothers, away from the colony. I love you. I'll understand if you don't want to go, but I want to do this."

He wrapped his arms around her. "Silly female. Where else would I be? As if I would stay on this planet without you. Who would say no to a life of adventure with his Pirate Queen?"

"Then it's settled then," she replied, snuggling into him.

"Goddess, I hope not. I don't think we're the settling kind."

She laughed with him—he was completely right. Neither of them was the settling type.

THE END

Afterword

T hank you so much for reading my novel! I am an Indie author, and reviews mean the world to us, so if you enjoyed this book, I'd love it if you could leave a review at https://mybook.to/WildF1 Re. If you want to share on social media, I'd love it if you can tag me at @rosemackieauthor on , or .

If you really loved it, and want to read more, check out where you can sign up for my newsletter to hear about future books (no spam, I promise). You'll get access to extra scenes, free novellas, and be the first to hear about new releases.

Colony 29, Phase 1 - Preliminary Survey Map.

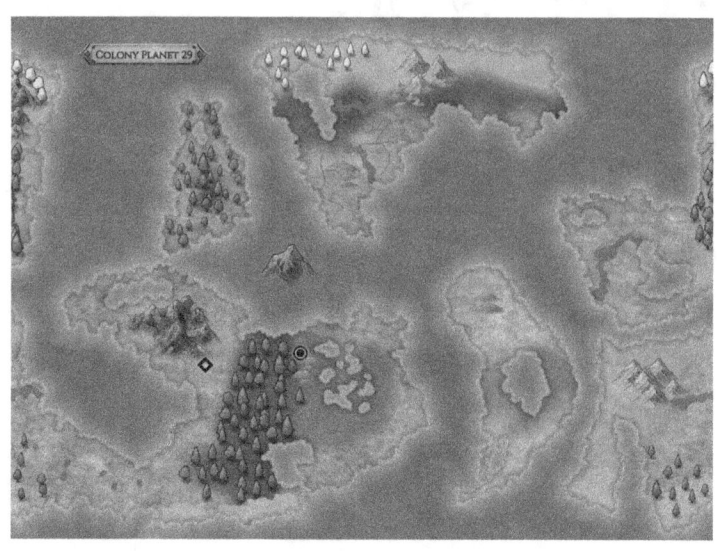

Legend: <> Crater   O Base Camp

Alliance Colonies

Colonial Alliance

The Colonial Alliance (referred to as the Alliance) was established when Earth started colonising other planets. Having undergone several shifts of focus during its hundreds of years, the current Alliance functions as an intergalactic council that governs non-human relationships, colonisation permits, interstellar travel, trade, banking and shared security concerns.

As Earth colonised nearby planets, in time, their colonies flourished and in turn created colonies of their own. This diaspora has created a complex network of colonies and history. In early colonisation, colonies were formed by businesses, countries, religions or communities of interest. The sudden availability of space to expand, and the technology to create suitable biospheres, has resulted in colonies and planets with distinct cultures and ideological differences. There was no need to compromise with your neighbour, when you could easily go establish a new colony with people that think like you. The colonies are fiercely independent and there is a delicate balance between shared interests and perceived infringement of colonial rights.

***

Planets (and associated interstellar objects) - Official Alliance Registry

Colonies are classified by the waves of colonisation in the Alliance history, and steps removed from Earth. Gen1 colonies were the first planets colonised by Earth. Gen2 are the colonies established by Earth's Gen1 colonies, and so on.

Earth: Home of the Alliance. Largely uninhabited due to planetary ecological rehabilitation measures; a flourishing eco-tourism destination.

- **Summer:** Gen1-1 Earth Colony. Wealthy, clean and heavily populated. Centre of Alliance business network.

  - **Winter:** Gen2-1 Summer Colony. Barely habitable, but generates significant amount of seafood that is expensive, has made those willing to live in the freezing conditions very wealthy.

    - **IntGal Supply 2:** Gen3-1 Winter Colony. An intergalactic trading and resupply station serving hundreds of races.

  - **Djilba:** Gen2-1 Summer Colony. A lush, fertile planet. Largely agrarian and well established, peaceful.

- **Farm Planet 2:** Gen3-1 Djilba Colony. Established as a farm planet to generate food and breed animals for interstellar trade. Highly successful. Very few inhabitants, mostly farmed with bots.

- **Victory:** Gen1-3 Earth Colony. Highly focussed on technology and research development and production, has damaged the biosphere significantly in the centuries since it was first established.

  - **Liberty:** Gen2-2 Victory Colony - FAILED. Colonists rebelled and tried to secede from Victory in dispute of the tithes on their income. Developed into a war, which damaged the biosphere; the planet remains largely uninhabitable.

  - **Destiny:** Gen2-1 Victory Colony. Moderately prosperous planet.

    - **Happy Water:** Gen3-2 Destiny Colony (although not strictly a colony). Water planet, minimal land masses. Farmed extensively for water. Water from this planet is considered to have significant health benefits.

    - **Farm Planet 1 (also called Where The Wild Bots Roam):** Gen3-1 Destiny Colony. Established as a farm planet to generate food and breed animals for interstellar trade. Highly successful. Very few inhabitants, mostly farmed with bots.

- **Nirvana:** Gen1-2 Earth Colony. Poor planet, invested heavily in the creation of colonies with minimal return. A cautionary tale for other colonies considering branching out; widely believed to be why there have been no recent colonies established.

  - **Haven:** Gen2-4 Nirvana Colony. Highly prosperous planet, unremarkable for any significant exports but many banks choose to base on Haven as it has low tithes.

    - **Ithrik Co:** Gen3-1 Haven Colony. Owned by the Ithrik corporation, makers of the Alliance's interstellar vehicle fleet. Guards the Talta system.

    - **Mining Association:** Gen3-3 Haven Colony. Not human habitable and unable to be terraformed. Owned by a Mining Association, planet extensively mined for mineral resources. Human-template species must remain within controlled bio-domes, any exposure to the atmosphere will kill within minutes.

  - **Zion:** Gen2-3 Nirvana Colony. A highly religious planet, home to a violent cult that rejects outsiders. Survives on fees for taking interstellar prisoners and managing Paradise.

    - **Paradise:** Gen3-1, Prison Planet.

  - **Valhalla:** Gen2-2 Nirvana Colony. A centre of trade for the Alliance, anything can be bought or sold on Valhalla. The small planet is covered in markets and bazaars.

- **LifeCo:** Gen3-1 Valhalla Colony. A tropical paradise holiday planet.

- **IntGal Supply 1:** Gen3-2 Valhalla Colony. An intergalactic trading and resupply station serving hundreds of races.

- **IntGal Explorer 1**: Gen3-3 Valhalla Colony. A deep space resupply station for exploration and survey vessels.

○ **Falosia:** Gen2-1 Nirvana Colony. A prosperous tropical planet with an 85% female population.

  - **Pandoria:** Gen3-1 Falosian Colony. A resources planet, mining has made Falosia rich. Very few inhabitants.

  - **IntGal Explorer 2:** Gen3-2 Falosian Colony. A deep space resupply station for exploration and survey vessels.

- **Pan:** Gen1-4 Earth Colony. Seceded after a prolonged war. A dangerous colony, ruled by criminal gangs

  ○ **Verit:** Gen2-1 Pan Colony. A freezing planet with a matriarchal society despite having a 80% male population. The most feared mercenaries in the alliance come from the Verit clans.

    - **VozMoz:** Gen3-1 Verit Colony. A harsh planet used as a training ground for soldiers from all over the

Alliance.

- **Colony 29:** Gen3-2 Verit / Falosian Joint Colony. Newly discovered world.

○ **Svoboda:** Gen2-2 Pan Colony. Considered an "enlightened" world with many universities, libraries and research facilities, Svobodans are widely known to be chauvinistic and are excellent spies. Their culture is highly politicised and they are active in guiding Alliance policy. They have extensively genetically altered their population, and as a result are long lived, exceeding 300 years.

○ **Uspekh:** Gen2-3 Pan Colony. A dangerous colony where armies and mercenaries can be hired.

- **Lief:** Gen3-1 Uspekh Colony. A largely uninhabitable planet populated by biodomes catering to extreme tastes. Despite being outlawed by the Alliance, there is a significant slave trade operating out of this colony.

Hierarchy

Falosia:

S'Daii: Alliance Delegate

K'Dec: Leader of Division or Colony

G'Dec/ Healer: Leader of field or speciality

V'Dec/ Specialist: Senior in a field

T-Dec: Officer

Y-Vet: Cadet or Young Adult

Ingen: children

Verit:

Matriarch: Leader of Verit

Maman: Member of the governing council of Verit

Prime: Male leader of a city/ tribe/ colony

-De: Leader of a field or speciality

-Pa: Second in command, senior officer

-Sa: Officer, young adult

-La: General reference for a trainee, child.

Note: Reference to a -La may also used to express dominance, addressing someone as -La indicates that you believe they are beneath you somehow.

***

Characters - Dalat Colony Personnel

Leadership

K'Dec Maral Lien: Governor of Colony 29, respected military leader, twin sister of S'Daii Delegate Amira Lien

Prime Frei Broun: Prime of the Dathalka Clan, assigned to Colony 29

Maman Frei Broun: Leader of the Dathalka Clan, active member of the Isolationist sect, observer for the Maman Council on Colony 29

Science and Medicine

Chief Healer Danara Pasal: respected medical leader, expertise in genetic research, Chief Healer Colony 29

Specialist Creen Rolla: Biological Researcher

Specialist Holly Frockman: Environmental Scientist

Specialist Amber Gentle: Genetic Engineer

Healer Fray Golden: Senior Medic

Specialist Livia Forlon: General Medic

Specialist Kirilee Alosi: Psychologist

Odran-De: Senior Healer, expert in biological adaptation of crops, Healer, child genius

Leife-Pa: Biochemist

Othre-Pa: Planetary Biologist

Paulus-Pa: Paramedic Nurse

Balfour-Pa: Surgery specialist

Kenan-Sa: Paramedic Nurse

Steffon-Pa: Physiotherapist

External Security

G'Dec Sraya Rattan: Defence Force Leader, Survivalist

T'Dec Ariel Swythe: Weapons specialist

V'Dec Brianne Wroth: Scanning technology specialist

Kren-Pa: Perimeter security specialist

Drue-Pa: Comms

Vordan-Pa: Pilot

Forden-Pa: Pilot

Rhodan-Pa: Cartographer

Internal Security

Lucius-De: First Warrior of the Dathalka Clan, assigned to lead the Warriors on Colony 29, leader of internal security

V'Dec Zera Garrick: Security Specialist

Tarlach-Sa: Security

T'Dec Lee Tyler: Security

Specialist Marianne Diaglo: Justice

Peyton-Pa: Justice and Security Officer

Logistics and Stores

G'Dec Lenora Pattra: Logistics and Stores Leader

T'Dec Yulli Fright: Logistics

Ilium-Pa: Pre-fab Building Specialist

Carrow-Sa: Pre-fab Building Specialist

Cuanaic-Sa: Pre-fab Building Specialist

Nythen-Pa: Pre-fab Buildings

T'Dec Olna Green: Food Storage

T'Dec Helena Yokine: Quartermaster

Gawan-Sa: Building Specialist

Eosaph-Sa: Nutritionist and Cook

T'Dec Dianal Joondan: Cook

Technology and Engineering
Broken-De: Head of Technology and Engineering
Rhein-Pa: Technical Engineer
Specialist Sara Flite: Comms Tech
Specialist Merna Rutha: Fabrication Tech
Specialist Grane Violet: Power Engineer
Specialist Rhian Freedit: Water Engineer
Offer-Pa: General systems specialist
Luken-De: Habitation Planner
Specialist Malika Renaldi: Construction Engineer
Sole-Pa: Construction Engineer
Vrue-Pa: Construction Engineer
Wilian-Pa: Machinery Maintenance
Menw-Sa: Machinery Maintenance
V'Dec Fila Maroo: Flora Specialist Engineer
Specialist Laila Dren: Horticultural Engineer
Specialist Rowen May: Horticultural Specialist
Specialist Trian Laferte: Fauna Specialist
Grayden-Pa: Flora Specialist
Brothrey-Pa: Fauna Specialist

Colony Administration
T'Dec Reen Olden: Administrator
Freiger-Pa: Colony Planner
Barram-Pa: Resource Manager

***

Characters - Others

S'Daii Delegate Amira Lien: Alliance Delegate responsible for Falosian colonial interests, twin sister to K'Dec Maral Lien

    Maman-La Bylelle: trainee of Maman Frei Broun, Dathalka Clan

    Maman-La Scara: trainee of Maman Frei Broun, Dathalka Clan

    Maman-Zelude: Head of Research, Maman Council, Aide to the Matriarch

    Amun: Denara Pasal's ex husband

    Varyn-De: First Male of Verit, mate to the Matriarch

    Matriarch-Rei: Leader of Verit

    Liara Lien: Deceased daughter of K'Dec Maral Lien, mother of Varis

    Varis: orphaned grand daughter of K'Dec Maral Lien

    Administrator Kevelan: Aide to S'Daii Delegate Amira Lien

    Adam Leask: Speaker of the Chamber, most senior member of the Alliance council, representative of Summer colony

    Nulium: Svobodan Ambassador to the Alliance, one third of the Alliance governor group

    Val-Huoz: Uspekh Ambassador to the Alliance, one third of the Alliance governor group

    Cui: Victory Ambassador to the Alliance, advisory board member, expert on ancient alien technology, Professor of Bio-Engineering and Archaeology

Maluriens

YouTre (Yut): Emperor of Maluria, Head of the Nuren Family

DuSar RuvasTyia (Ruya): Deceased first mate of DuSin Maken-Roy, Ambassador to the Alliance for the Malurien Empire, part of the Nuren Family, the family of the current Emperor

Dusar MavenSul (Mavi): Nuren family Head of Alliances and Negotiations, younger sister of the current Emperor of Maluria, aunt of DuSin MakenRoy, Ambassador to the Alliance for the Malurien Empire, part of the Nuren Family, the family of the current Emperor

DuSin CromJut (Cromu): Head of security for the Nuren family, mate of DuSan MavenSul, part of the Nuren Family

DuniyaLo (Duni or Duniya): Trainee in the Nuren family diplomatic team, reporting to DuSar MavenSul, recently promoted, part of the Nuren Family

DuSin MakenRoy (Maku): Ambassador to the Alliance for the Malurien Empire, part of the Nuren Family, nephew of the current Emperor

SirutYua (Siru): Commander of the Malurien Embassy security detachment on Summer, part of the Nuren Family, the family of the current Emperor, cousin to DuSin MakenRoy on his father's side

HualYor (Hulo): eldest son of DuSin MakenRoy, part of the Nuren Family, the family of the current Emperor

SadutVir (Sadu): youngest son of DuSin MakenRoy, part of the Nuren Family, the family of the current Emperor

Loren JidurYut (Jidu): Commander of the Malurien external security forces, mate to the Gustana BuyaRen, part of the Nuren Family, the family of the current Emperor

Gustana BuyaRen (Buya): Supreme commander of the Malurien military, eldest sister of the current Emperor, mother of DuSin MakenRoy, mate of Loren JidurYut, part of the Nuren Family

Hidden Fire (Under Violet Suns Book 4)

Hidden Fire: A Sci FI Alien Romance (Under Violet Suns Book 4) - Order Now on Amazon at https://mybook.to/HiddenFireRoseMackie

Would you trade your life to the alien prince, to save your planet?

Maral is the leader a new colony that represents the survival for two planets. She is responsible for the colony success, and all the souls that have taken the risk of moving there. However, they are all in danger. They desperately need the assistance of the alien Maluriens to protect themselves.

MakenRoy, Prince of the Maluriens, is willing to offer his help...on one condition. He wants Maral.

What to expect: Glorious world building and a sweet, steamy sci-fi, alien romance. Hidden Fire is a full-length, enemies-to-lovers romance. The Under Violet Suns series has a progressive story, but each book is a complete HEA adventure with no cliff-hanger.

Read on for an excerpt from Hidden Fire.

Chapter 1: A Proposition

Maral paced the corridor in front of the guest quarters in a vain attempt to burn off her nervous energy. What she was about to do was the riskiest thing she had ever attempted, and a persistent voice in her head insisted that it was a terrible idea. She mostly agreed with her inner voice, but was clear-sighted enough to realize that there were simply no other viable options.

Here, in this quiet corridor, she could indulge in her anxiety where no one could see her. To everyone else, she must be the K'Dec. Governor of the colony, leader in the Falosian military. But here, in this stolen slice of silence, she could just be Maral, facing the most challenging mission of her life. The future of multiple planets could rest on her pulling off this negotiation.

Maral sighed. When the shit hits the fan, and you accept that all the choices you have are bad ones, it brings a chilling clarity. She took a

deep breath, accepting the decision before her, and entered the guest
wing. The complex was nearly empty, only a single guest currently
visiting their little colony.

After the recent sabotage, impending war, and facilities that could
only generously be called 'rustic', people weren't exactly lining up
outside to visit. Yet. When word got out about what they had discovered here... *No. One problem at a time.*

When she approached the only occupied room, the bored security
personnel stationed outside the door perked up visibly. She nodded
politely at them and pressed the buzzer to request entry.

After a momentary delay, the door swished open to reveal the
imposing figure of MakenRoy, Alliance Ambassador and Malurien
Royal. He was also the male that she had welcomed as a 'guest' several
weeks ago, and was now preventing from leaving. To say that he was
not pleased was an understatement. He was a persistent pain in her
ass.

The only thing that gave her even the slightest hope that she could
pull off the audacious plan that the leaders of Verit and Falosia had
concocted was that the male was still here. Maluriens were dangerous,
and MakenRoy was no exception. They were known as politicians,
spies, and occasional assassins across the galaxy. If he wanted to escape
custody, he could. Her colony was largely unexplored and uninhabited. He could easily escape and hide in the woods, waiting for rescue. Or
pick them off one by one if they were foolish enough to try to reacquire
him. No, he was still here because he wanted something. Pissing her
off was just a bonus, a way for him to pass the time. A way to extract
some small measure of retribution for his imprisonment.

"Good afternoon, K'Dec. This is a surprise." His voice was deep
and rich, giving nothing away behind the polite façade. So, it was the
Ambassador she was meeting today. Not one of his other personas that

he seemed to change with the ease that other people changed clothing. He was smooth. She had to give him that. The moment they had captured him, he had shed his affable image for this one. Charming, silky-smooth politician manners that hid everything.

She was reluctantly impressed. Not even the barest hint of his emotions or thoughts leaked out. Maral was one of the strongest empaths Falosia had ever produced, one of the rare dual telepaths, and she hadn't caught even a whisper of his feelings. It spoke to an iron control that few people possessed. It was slowly driving her nuts. She hadn't realized how much she had come to rely on her additional senses until they were useless. It made her tread carefully in her dealings with him, expecting a poisonous barb at each juncture.

"My apologies for interrupting your afternoon." She paused, waiting for him to respond. He simply stared at her impassively. *Okay then.* She smiled at him, launching her own charm offensive. "May I come in? I have a matter I would like to discuss with you."

He blinked in surprise at her saccharine sweetness before frowning deeply. Clearly, he wasn't buying her act any more than she was buying his. After weeks of this stalemate, she wasn't exactly surprised. "Of course, K'Dec. It's not like I have much else to do." He bared his red tipped fangs at her in a facsimile of a smile, and stepped back, sweeping his hand into the room, the sharp black horns and talons on his hands glinting in the light.

The unit was exactly the same as the other sixty or so on the planet. A simple cabin, featuring a bed, a small kitchenette and seating area, an entertainment screen, and a small toilet and closet off to the side. It was functional and bland, everything in the same uniform gray.

MakenRoy looked huge in the small space, as he motioned her to take a seat at the little table while he perched on the end of the bed. He said nothing, just waited for her to speak. A huge hulking gray-skinned male covered in sharp ridges of cartilage and bone.

She supposed she deserved his reticence. She was detaining him. He was a prisoner here. He was not fooled by this little unit. It was not a guest suite; it was a jail.

"My apologies for keeping you here so long, Ambassador. We have been proceeding with our investigations in relation to your involvement with the military force that attacked us from your transport ship."

He cocked his head, his red eyes staring at her unblinkingly. "Have your extensive and lengthy investigations concluded?" His tone was caustic.

She didn't rise to the bait, and continued in her calm, methodical manner. "We have determined Svoboda's culpability. The attacks and sabotage have been part of a carefully orchestrated plan by them to take possession of this planet."

He blinked. It was only for a split second, but in his controlled countenance, it practically screamed at her.

"How unexpected," he murmured. "To what end? This planet is appealing in its own rugged way, but Svoboda is highly advanced. They have their own colonies. I am aware of their cultural enmity for your gender, but this endeavor appears rash, and Svobodans are not fools. It would be a logistical nightmare for them to hold this planet, and it would alienate many worlds."

Maral realized partway through his monologue that he wasn't actually talking to her. He was thinking aloud, his eyes distant. His eyes focused on her, flaring a darker red. "There are only two options. You are engaged in some other form of warfare with Svoboda, of which this is the most recent salvo. That is unlikely. My spies are the best in the universe, and we have heard nothing of this. The second option is that you have something they want on this planet." He nodded decisively; his jaw clenched. "That's it. What have you discovered? What is it on this planet that makes it worth the effort and risk for them?"

Maral forced herself to remain calm as her heart rate spiked. MakenRoy had deduced, just from a few sentences of information, what had taken weeks of careful investigation. She silently reassessed him and upped his already sky-high threat assessment. He was fiercely intelligent. She would have to tread carefully in this next step. The stakes were too high.

"You are correct. There is something on this planet that they want." She paused, balanced on a knife edge. She had the strangest sensation that the universe was holding its breath, waiting for her next words. There was no going back from this. It had to work. If he didn't agree, she couldn't let him leave this planet alive. "This planet is rich in natural Zyilan."

His eyes flared again–it was mesmerizing, like a cobra. She watched him, his brain feverishly calculating the staggering implications. His body thrummed with tension, and she could see that he wanted to pace, but there was no room in the unit. Every warning in her empathic senses tripped; he was so agitated that she felt his thoughts like static in the air, irritating her exposed skin.

Eventually, he spoke. Unexpectedly, he didn't explode or exclaim as she would have expected. His control was astonishing. "I see. That does put things in perspective." He cocked his head at her. "What do you want, K'Dec?"

Perversely, his iron control needled at her. When you are told that you are sitting on a planet where the rarest mineral in the galaxy has just been discovered in massive quantities, a little reaction would be normal. Whoever owned this planet could be a new emperor in the galaxy. She cocked her head at him, determined to get a rise. "Why do you think I want anything?"

He snorted. "Please, don't take me for one of your slow-witted barbarian Verit. You want something, something you think you can only get by trading this information. If I don't agree, you'll try to kill me."

He wasn't wrong, either in his assessment of their Verit allies, or his precarious situation. He sat back, lacing the horns on his hands over his knuckles, and waited for her response. How he could remain so calm when they were discussing murdering him was beyond her.

"We intend to confront the Alliance with Svoboda's wrongdoing. We hope they will take action when presented with the evidence we have gathered."

He stared at her intently, his unblinking eyes alien on her. It felt like staring at a snake.

"You don't think they will." His voice was flat.

She hesitated and shook her head. "We suspect that the Alliance has been infiltrated. The information they had on our shipments, the troops arriving on your ship... it all hints at infiltration across several departments and levels. Maybe even the council itself. No, we don't expect the Alliance to do anything."

"What does that have to do with me?"

"The Alliance is not the only galactic conglomerate. The only other known natural source of Zyilan is in Alliance space. For the past two centuries, non-human species have complained about the xenophobic restrictions placed on the sale of Zyilan by the Alliance. If the Alliance does not intercede to stop Svoboda, our colony plus Verit, Falosia, and their subsidiary colonies and stations, will secede from the Alliance. We will need allies."

MakenRoy lunged forward and seized her wrist in an iron grip. She tried to pull away, and he hissed at her, baring his fangs. "Be calm. I will not harm you. I must know whether you speak the truth." He pushed up the wrist of her jumpsuit and placed his fingers on her pulse point. His fingers were rough, shackling her. He did not hurt her, but his grip was unyielding, and so hot it was just short of burning her skin.

The K'Dec bared her teeth, fury flooding her, and pulled her gun with her other hand. She held the deadly little pulse pistol to his head. "That was unwise, Malurien," she hissed. "If you make any further aggressive actions, I will shoot you and deal with the consequences later."

He laughed derisively, and she saw a feral light enter his eyes. He was enjoying this! The crass asshole wanted to fight with her, was getting a kick out of her holding a gun to his head. "No, you won't. Your people need me" His arrogance set her teeth on edge.

"They'll be annoyed at me, certainly. But you are not the only alien group we could make our offer to, Malurien. If you say no, I will have to shoot you anyway." She shrugged. "They never need to know that you were shot just because you annoyed me."

Shockingly, the infuriating male grinned at her, appreciation heating his eyes further. He leaned into her space. "I like this side of you, K'Dec. You should let it out more."

"You opinion of any side of me is irrelevant." Silently, she kicked herself. What kind of comeback was that? She used the butt of the gun to push him back slightly. "Behave. Why have you grabbed my wrist?"

He sighed dramatically and shook his head at her in mock disappointment. "I told you. I need to be assured of your veracity. Be specific, K'Dec. What do you offer?"

Maral took a deep breath, pulling herself back into business mode. She couldn't let herself by distracted in such an important moment by his antics. "If we secede from the Alliance, we offer to enter a commercial and military trade agreement with the Malurien Empire. In exchange for preferential trade agreements and access to Zyilan, you will provide us with military and logistical support against the Alliance. We will establish the Dalat colony as an open trade planet, where all species can trade for Zyilan."

He stilled, his jaw clenched, judging her sincerity. The tension stretched out between them. "I do not have the authority to enter such an agreement." Disappointment was bitter in her mouth. "However, I can agree in principle. The negotiations will require the involvement of several of the Malurien senior ministers. We will need to travel to Maluria to complete the negotiations."

The K'Dec nodded, relief making her light-headed. She had killed before for her people, and would again, but she found she was relieved that she didn't need to kill this male. Taking a life should never be casual or easy. Maral nodded brusquely, hiding her emotions, and stood, preparing to leave. She couldn't wait to get out of the small space. She hated this, all of it. She was a general and a warrior, not a politician. "This is acceptable. I will convey your acceptance to Ambassador S'Daii Amira. She will liaise with your people to progress to the next stage."

She tried to step away, but he refused to release her wrist. Maken-Roy smiled at her. A genuine one this time, she thought, displaying even more of his large fangs. "We are not finished yet. What happens if the Alliance intercedes? What becomes of our agreement then?"

The K'Dec sank back down into her chair. "If the Alliance intercedes, we will stay under Alliance rule. They will have a purview over Zyilan transactions. We will be unable to enter an agreement. In that instance, I am authorized to offer you a gift of ten grams of Zyilan, in thanks for considering our offer, and as an apology for your extended stay here."

MakenRoy barked a shocked laugh. Ten grams of Zyilan could buy an entire military fleet, or a planet somewhere. "I accept the terms, K'Dec. I have two more of my own." Maral nodded, waiting to see what he would try to extort. "First, I want out of this accommodation unit. If you wish to enter into a Malurien alliance, you must learn to trust us."

Maral considered. It was only fair. It went against every bone in her body to let a dangerous individual wander freely around her colony, but he was right. They had to start somewhere. "Fine, but you will still have guards. Trust is earned."

He flashed another smile at her. "Agreed."

"I'm not finished. You may not leave the compound."

He scowled. "I am not one of your tame Verit cats. I will not be held here against my will." She could feel the anger steaming off of him.

"I am responsible for this deal, MakenRoy, and this colony's safety. I will not risk you escaping into the wilderness."

He didn't respond. After a long moment, he huffed and shook his head. "Second, I wish to know who you present for your Alliance. Will it be yourself? The S'Daii?"

It was Maral's turn to frown. "I'm sorry, I don't understand."

MakenRoy sighed. "I suspected as much. You have done no research into Malurien culture, have you?"

Maral stiffened in affront. "I have. The Malurien empire, governed by the Malurien royal family. The Empire comprises dozens of different planets and species. Extensive commercial interests, extending well beyond human-controlled space, and advanced military capabilities. No significant sentient rights sanctions."

He smiled at her, pleased. Human-template species were notoriously xenophobic and rarely bothered to learn about other cultures. "Maluriens are a communal species. The core of our society is community; family, friendship, home–these things bind us. They take precedence over all other considerations and contracts. To enter an alliance of this magnitude, which may require military action against the human Alliance, you are asking for the highest level of trust and connection. It will need to be sealed with a mating. There is no other way we can intervene, as we already have a non-aggression pact with the Alliance."

Maral's stomach dropped into her shoes. In all her research, she had not come across this as a potential issue. MakenRoy continued. "However, if the planet of one of our own royal mates was threatened, it would supersede our non-aggression pact. We would not attack the Alliance, but we would defend our own. The Alliance themselves would be in breach, by attacking it, as they have pledged in the treaty not to attack any Malurien planet." He leaned forward, his elbows balanced on his knees. "I ask you again, who do you propose for the mating?"

Maral swallowed, her mouth dry, her stomach sick. "I will need to discuss and come back to you. We had not considered this aspect of your culture. It will require some debate."

MakenRoy regarded her frankly for a moment. "Very well. Don't take too long deciding. The mate will need to be approved by my family as well."

Maral forced numb lips to move. "Who would be the Malurien that our representative would bond with?"

MakenRoy looked at her as if she was stupid. "This is my negotiation. I have no mate presently. I will be the Malurien mate for this arrangement."

Maral's stomach dropped. What insane female would mate with this male? He was dangerous, unpredictable and changed personality on a whim. The poor female would be mad within a week.

Her brain caught up with what he had just said. "Presently? So, your matings can be time fixed? Falosians generally only mate for five years at a time." Perhaps it wouldn't be so challenging. Surely there would be a suitable female willing to enlist in this service for five years. Maluriens may not be human-template, but they were attractive enough. They were close enough to human anatomy; bi-pedal, mammalian, similar enough features. Apart from being larger, hairless, gray skinned, horned, and taloned, there were not that many apparent physical differences.

He sighed, the fire in his eyes dimming slightly. "No, Malurien mating is permanent. My last mate, RuvasTyia, died. I have not taken another since."

Maral felt the first flicker of emotion from him, an echo of sadness. Just a hint that had made its way through his formidable shields. "I see." She paused. "This will present a challenge. Few Falosians would bind permanently to a male they do not know. Verit even less so—they rarely bond to a single partner longer than the period necessary to produce offspring."

MakenRoy shrugged, clearly indicating that such concerns were not his problem. "If you wish the alliance to proceed, then you will find a solution. The female must be of sufficient seniority and authority to match mating a Malurien royal such as myself. She will be a *DuSar* after the mating, after all." He grinned broadly and raised his chin arrogantly at her. "Make her impressive, K'Dec."

She rolled her eyes and rose to stand. "I will see what I can find, Ambassador."

She opened the door and stepped out, motioning him to follow
her. The Falosian guards instantly snapped to attention. "The Ambassador is granted permission to move around the colony, provided
he is accompanied by a guard. He may not exit the compound."

"Acknowledged, Ma'am," the guards chorused.

Maral turned back to MakenRoy, looming in the doorway. "You
may leave your quarters as you see fit. I will make the arrangements for
us to travel to the Alliance home world in the next few days."

She hesitated, feeling that so many things were left unsaid between
them, then turned to leave. He remained silent, his red eyes following
her as she exited back across the compound to her offices.

***

Maral settled into her chair before her desk and exhaled deeply. The
first part was done, despite the Malurien throwing them all a curve ball
they hadn't seen coming. Still, their hand was played, and they had got
the outcome they wanted, mostly.

She placed a call to her sister, Ambassador S'Daii Amira. Amira was
the Falosian delegate to the Alliance, and the mastermind behind this
crazy, bold plan.

"This is Administrator Kevelan of the Falosian Embassy on Summer."

Maral sighed. She and Kevelan, Amira's bulldog of an assistant,
did not get on. He guarded his mistress's time fiercely, and had been
known to stall for days if he didn't like someone. "Kevelan, it's Maral.
Please put me through to Amira."

"Yes, K'Dec. Immediately."

Maral blinked in surprise. The universe must be coming to an end
for Kevelan to put her through without a fight. She waited just a few
seconds before Amira's face filled the transparent display screen, so

familiar to her own. Hardly surprising, given they were twins. "Maral, the line is secure. Did he agree?"

"He did."

Amira exhaled gustily. This had been the most uncertain part of the plan. Amira did not smile. She knew Maral well enough to know she was hiding something. "But?"

"To seal the deal, they want a senior Falosian or a senior Verit female to mate with MakenRoy. They have a non-aggression pact with the Alliance. The only way they can break it is if they are defending the planet of a family member."

Amira didn't flinch, decades of navigating the murky politics of the Alliance giving her an immutable calm. "I see. Well, this is unexpected, but not unsurmountable."

Maral was aghast at her flippant attitude. "Is that all? We are asking some poor unsuspecting female to mate permanently with an alien. For what? For-"

"For the sake of our species. For the sake of our planet, and our people!" Amira snapped. "Don't be so provincial, Maral. You know full well that people mate for all kinds of reasons, all the time, with all sorts of species. Love, offspring, security, money, power... people do things for whatever they care about most. If my understanding of Malurien culture is right, MakenRoy's mate will become a *DuSar*, a member of the royal family. She will be incredibly powerful. She will spend her life in luxury, while saving her people. It's not exactly a hardship."

"So, we'll force some female to mate-"

Amira cut her off again. "Who said we'd force anyone? We are not Svoboda to enchain females, or selfish Maman to push people about the chessboard to our own designs. We will simply ask if any of our trusted senior personnel would consider this assignment."

Maral sighed, still unhappy, but forced to concede that Amira was right. This was why Amira had become an ambassador, while she'd been happy in the military. Maral had often been told that her thinking was too rigid for politics, too black and white, unwilling to compromise, to understand that the world was full of gray. She had been perfectly happy as the commander of a space station, before she had been assigned here to Dalat colony. This was meant to be a quiet posting, but it had turned into the most challenging station in the Falosian military.

Shaking off her frustration, she got the discussion back on track. "We can be ready to join you on Summer any day now. Can you organize it, please?"

Amira grinned. "Very well. I have a ship on standby. They will be there within a day to pick you and MakenRoy up."

They finished up their pleasantries and ended the call. After, Maral sat in her office, gazing out the window, considering how her life had brought her to such a strange place. She had been Falosian military most of her seventy years, as had her mother before her. For a Falosian, it wasn't all that long. Her people typically lived two or three hundred years; she wasn't even middle-aged yet. But she felt ancient, worn down by the demands of the life she had chosen.

As she had worked her way up the ranks, she had fought for her planet and her people all across the galaxy. Never had she imagined that she would end up as governor on a backwater planet that was suddenly the center of an interstellar conflict, negotiating an alliance with an alien royal. The Goddess certainly had a sense of humor.

Maral watched the activity on the green. From her office on the ground floor of the colony admin building, she could see the expanse of the open green square, across to the rec center and mess hall on the other side.

She loved watching the colonists interact. Every day, she saw more signs of their budding community, their integration. She was coldly furious and deeply sad that this daring venture they had embarked on may be overtaken by Svobodan machinations. This planet had been meant as a mating planet, a place where Verit and Falosian colonists could find mates, and revive their declining birth-rates. Instead, it had become the nexus of a conflict spanning the known galaxy. What would become of her people if this colony failed?

She watched MakenRoy exit the gym. She waited a few moments longer, then cursed when she realized the guards were not following him. He strolled around the corner of the rec building, ducking between the buildings and into the darkness. She sprang out of her chair and raced after him and placed a call to her second in command, Sraya.

"The Malurien has escaped. He's headed into the woods, and knows about the Zyilan." She heard Sraya's intake of breath. "Find out what happened to the guards. I'm following MakenRoy. Send a detachment after me."

"Acknowledged," came the clipped response.